S0-AGQ-703

KILLERS

Our Lady of
the River's Mouth

NICOLE M. TAYLOR

EPIC
Press

SCOTT COUNTY LIBRARY SYSTEM
Hdqrs: 200 N. 6th Avenue
ELDRIDGE, IA 52748

Our Lady of the River's Mouth
Killers

Written by Nicole M. Taylor

Copyright © 2017 by Abdo Consulting Group, Inc.

Published by EPIC Press™
PO Box 398166
Minneapolis, MN 55439

All rights reserved.

Printed in the United States of America.

International copyrights reserved in all countries.
No part of this book may be reproduced in any form without
written permission from the publisher. EPIC Press™ is trademark
and logo of Abdo Consulting Group, Inc.

Cover design by Christina Doffing
Images for cover art obtained from iStockPhoto.com
Edited by Jennifer Skogen

LIBRARY OF CONGRESS CATALOGING-IN-PUBLICATION DATA

Names: Taylor, Nicole M., author.
Title: Our lady of the river's mouth / by Nicole M. Taylor.
Description: Minneapolis, MN : EPIC Press, 2017. | Series: Killers
Summary: A truck-stop waitress partners with a psychic, a ghost, and her old high-school-
     flame-turned-sheriff's-deputy to find out who has been murdering women and dumping
     them in the woods around her small town.
 Identifiers: LCCN 2016946206 | ISBN 9781680764888 (lib. bdg.) |
     ISBN 9781680765441 (ebook)
Subjects: LCSH: Murderers—Fiction. | Murder—Investigation—Fiction. | Detectives—
     Fiction. | Mystery and detective stories—Fiction. | Young adult fiction.
Classification: DDC [Fic]—dc23
LC record available at http://lccn.loc.gov/2016946206

EPICPRESS.COM

For Poor Ellen Smith, Little Sadie, Delia,
and all of those who went unsung

Forest Interlude

1

Retrace your way? No, never!

These woods no more you'll roam

So bid farewell forever

To parents, friends and home

    —*The Ballad of Pearl Bryant, traditional*

I watched, from outside, from an uncertain distance, as he wrestled me into position with some difficulty. He took no particular care with me; if my head bumped on the uneven ground or my fingers snagged on the underbrush, he didn't notice.

His eyes were just staring, like when you're so tired you can't will yourself to look away from something. But it wasn't me he was looking at.

Even when he got me out where he felt safe—a

big elm bending its branches over the two of us—it still didn't look like he was really seeing me. I had become another feature of the earth, like a strange root system that was bursting up through the ground. My hair was the same color as the dirt. My skin was the color of the grubs that tunneled inside it.

He lowered himself onto me and I imagined what that weight felt like. I tried to conjure up the feeling of pressure and human warmth and the occasional gusts of breath. What had his breath smelled like? Coffee? Sardines? Morning-stink?

I had never seen it like this before, from above and far away. This pathetic scrambling.

It was stupid to feel embarrassed, ashamed for whatever of myself was left in that body. But some part of me wanted to turn around and look away, spare myself, I guess? Another part—a bigger part— knew that it was important that I stay here and that I see everything. I was a witness. My only witness.

He stopped after just a few moments. Whatever he wanted to do, it wasn't working. He sat back on his heels and I could see myself clearly, lying there with my face turned up toward God and everybody.

From a distance, it was easy to see that my left eyebrow was less tweezed than the right and my nose had a bump in it more pronounced than I remembered. There was a scar on my upper arm, about an inch or so long and perfectly straight, like someone had measured it out with a level. It looked old, dull beige instead of pink, and it must have been deep at one time. I wondered where I had gotten it.

I was also white, the whitest I had ever been, probably. A white that shaded into blue, the kind of color a live person never had. My mouth was open, but not like I was sleeping, more like a hole in my face, the way old people look when they take out their false teeth. All of those were things that death changes, and I understood that.

What I didn't understand was that scar. It was right there, plainly visible. How was it that I was seeing it now for the first time? The more I stared at that scar and the skin around it, the less I recognized it. It was like seeing a picture of yourself and not being able to match it up to the face in the mirror.

That girl on the ground looked like she could have been a cousin to me, a sister even. She could have been, but she wasn't.

The man rooted around in the undergrowth until he found a little branch that he took to me with a doctor's detachment. It was like I was a formaldehyde frog, all pinned open for him to poke at curiously.

All I could think was: *can't you see there's nothing left of me there?*

As he labored over me, posing me just right like someone fussing with a store mannequin in a window display, I couldn't help but think about how little I had been. Not how fat or skinny I was, I mean how *little* my body was, all things considered. It seemed suddenly incredible to believe that everything I ever was had once fit inside there.

One of my shoes was missing. Where did it go?

He rose to his knees to examine his work, tilting

his head to one side like he was hanging a picture frame on the wall. He grabbed one of my ankles and pulled my leg up and out until it was bent and turned open to anyone who came by.

He moved me like he was following a map that only existed in his own head. I could hear his breathing and how it had changed. It was slightly faster now, and deeper, which might have been from exertion. When he was pleased with the position of my limbs, he took my head in both of his hands and moved it, first to the left and then the right, but neither of those positions seemed to make him happy. He tilted it back until the top of my skull rested against the tree's bark and the new red welt on my throat was pointed up toward the sky.

I could remember it mostly as a feeling, of something pressing in on my throat and the darkness at the edge of my vision and the panic and desperation, the air that wouldn't come. But I never *saw* it before. It was surprisingly thin, just a little spindly line and it looked like a deep bruise. It didn't look like something that would kill a person.

I had expected all of this to be so different. I expected it to be . . . *more*. I was used to life disappointing me but I guess I still expected more from death. It reminded me of being fifteen and still waiting on my period, years after it had happened to all my friends. When it finally came on me, it was a surprise. I didn't feel strange or sick at all, I just looked down and saw the toilet filling up with red. I was delighted for about a minute—finally! I could say I was a real woman! But then the bleeding didn't stop.

I had imagined that it would be like a nosebleed, only from my crotch. I was not prepared for the stabs of pain, like a fist clenching inside of me, or more importantly, for the strange things that I produced. Clumps of tissue, a black-purple color rather than the normal red issued from me at an alarming rate.

Something was wrong. I had gone too long

before getting my period and something had gone off inside me, like milk curdling in the jug. I was rotting. The proof was in the pain, was in the strange, semi-solid pieces falling out of me. How could this be anything other than a part of my body, something I needed to stay alive?

When I didn't have any other options, I went to my mother. I told her what was happening and that I should probably go to the hospital. "Big pieces of me are . . . coming out," I said.

She rolled her eyes at me and took my arm in her hands, rubbing it vigorously in a modified Indian-burn. "Look," she said, pointing at the ghostly cloud of skin particles that caught the light and spun upward from my wounded arm. "Pieces of you. Your body does it all the time."

From then on, I thought of the thing between my legs as its own kind of cold-blooded animal—a thing that sheds and expels itself. It wasn't until about a year later, when I went on birth control, that I figured out that my mom was wrong as usual.

My doctor said it was endometriosis and all my suffering had been for nothing.

It occurred to me that, though I could remember my conversation with her clearly, I couldn't conjure up anything else about my mother. I didn't remember her name or what her face looked like or how she smelled. I remembered very clearly, though, that feeling of something drifting away from me. One last piece, battered maybe and small certainly, of my little-kid delusion that my mother was a source of knowledge and guidance.

Here I was again, looking around for the things that everyone else had—the normal, natural things that were supposed to come to me but never seemed to, until suddenly they did and it was all suffering and fear.

He stood up and plucked a leaf out of my hair—leaving behind a half-dozen others, crumbled in amongst the tangled strands—and looked around at the empty forest.

For the first time, he seemed to see and recognize

what was in front of him. He had a fat, sated look on his face, like he'd just finished a big old Thanksgiving dinner. He turned back to me and, after a few moments of contemplation, spit on my body.

The spit landed on my shoulder and tracked a snail-trail down my chest. Something about that must have felt like an ending to him, because he turned and headed back the way he had dragged me, toward his truck.

I realized that he was leaving me there, leaving me to the animals and the bugs. He was the last person who was ever going to look at me, the last person who was ever going to see me. I was going to be alone.

I could not stand the thought of that—being alone with the silence of the trees and no one ever knowing, no one ever seeing me. There wasn't even going to be a marker or a sign, nothing to say who I was or what I had done or what had been done to me.

So I followed him. He was the last witness, the last person who knew my name and where I came from, where I ended up. I stuck to his side like a shy child, following him back to the fire road where he had parked his truck.

I positioned myself in his shotgun seat while he climbed up behind the wheel. Wherever he went from then on, I would be there too. When he turned the key in the ignition, the radio boomed out, way louder than either of us were expecting. I saw him jolt a little and then he smiled, chuckling at himself the way anyone did when they caught themselves in a moment of ridiculousness. After all, what did he have to be afraid of?

In the same way that I could not conjure up an image of my mother's face or recall exactly where I had met the man who killed me, I had no memory of getting out of the truck. Yet, I found myself on foot again, deep in the trees. Over my shoulder was the clearing where my body rested, a few feet away was the fire road. I could see his tire tracks in the soft, dry dirt.

So I started walking, following his tracks toward the highway. I was not afraid of losing him. He was driving, true, but I could walk forever if I wanted to.

Again, I followed the fire road all the way to where it met the highway. Or where it should have met the highway. Instead of thinning trees and the noise of passing cars, I just found more trees, deeper trees and, eventually, the now-familiar tree where my body was. I had walked a loop somehow.

The girl on the ground looked up beyond me into the blue sky. With her face turned away like that and her eyes—my eyes—impossible to see, it seemed like maybe she was just looking at something awfully riveting up there, something no one else had noticed.

But when I turned my head, all I could see was the sky. And even that looked like rain was coming in. The clouds in the distance were gray-bottomed and rolling slow. I sighed and leaned over the girl on the ground and stretched my arms and torso over her tangled hair and upturned face. It was little protection but it was better than nothing. At least, I hoped it was better than nothing.

We waited together for the rain.

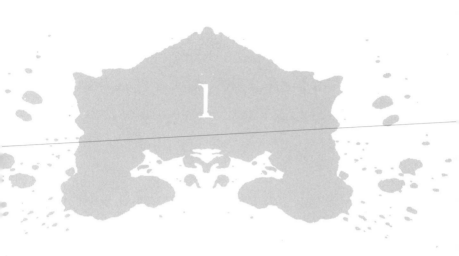

1

Blue and red lit up my mirror about a half mile from the diner and I knew for sure I wasn't speeding. Sure enough, the lights arced around me and into the other lane. I couldn't help but wonder if they had found another dead girl.

The first one turned up almost three years ago, my junior year of high school, and she wasn't much older than me. Back then, they thought—we all thought—that was the only one we'd ever find. They called her Jane Doe, though that was supposed to be just a stop-gap name until we could find her real one.

Next, they found the sisters, called Sandy Doe for the color of her hair and Skipper Doe, because that was Barbie's little sister. The fourth one was actually the first one killed, or so they thought. They called her Minnie Doe because she had one of those plastic barrettes that kids wear in her pocket with Minnie Mouse on it.

Queenie Doe got her name from the crown she had tattooed on her upper arm. She was number five, found the week I graduated from high school.

They started scouring the state forest that nearly encircled the town. Folks would go out and help them look, arms hooked together like they were playing Red Rover. Found eleven in all, but it had been quiet for about a year now.

There were seven miles between the diner and my place and, sure enough, at mile six I saw them. The woods were too deep for me to make out much, just flickers of red and blue.

Gramma's house—well, I suppose it was mine now—was at the far end of a long drive, far from anything else you might call human habitation. It was surrounded by cornfields on three sides and the state forest on the fourth. Spitting distance.

Trees my great-grandfather had planted grew up on either side of the drive and made it feel like you were taking a secret tunnel down into some dark cave. From my front porch, I couldn't even see the lights of the highway. And now, I couldn't help but think there was someone—some stranger—out there in *my* woods where I used to make stick forts and catch frogs, leaving human beings behind like they were garbage. If he was standing in the right spot, he could probably see the lights from my kitchen window while he did it.

When I got inside Peter and Aleph were looking at me, their little ink-drop eyes expectant as they stood up against the corner of their cage. I tapped my tongue against the roof of my mouth, making a little *schu-schu-schu* sound as I reached into the cage to grab Aleph. He liked to hide in the folds of my clothes while I puttered around the house. I let him scramble up the arm of my uniform, nosing curiously underneath my collar as I gave Peter's belly a vigorous scratching. Peter had always been the more standoffish one, the more dignified of the two. I took Aleph into the kitchen with me to evaluate the prospects for dinner. There wasn't much in the fridge—diner leftovers from day-before-last, ketchup and mustard and a Budweiser tallboy from the last time Devon visited, which had to have been more than a year ago.

The kitchen was to the side of the house, facing toward the woods, and I had spent many a boring meal searching the tree line for a rustle of animals—red foxes and the long, tapered heads of white-tail deer. I paused now, squinting to see if I could make out police lights through the endless sea of trees. But there was nothing, just the textured darkness of the tree limbs against the moonlit night.

Aleph was getting antsy, kept trying to scramble down my back, so I shut the fridge and put him back in his cage with Peter. "Should we see what's on the TV?"

I was sleeping on the sofa because, toward the end, Gramma needed tending all through the night and I couldn't hear her if I was upstairs.

There was nothing on TV except a few movies and a lot of infomercials. Probably even the local news stations didn't know yet about the . . . whatever it was out in the forest.

Out of the corner of my eye, I could see into Gramma's room. I could see the shadowy contours of the special medical bed we had to buy and her skeletal IV, the oxygen machine on the floor with its cord wrapped around it like a tail. Before she died, I would have given anything for a moment without the sputtering sighs of the oxygen machine and her own tortured breathing, but now the silence laid on me like an unsupportable burden.

I wondered if the cops were still out in the forest. I wondered if there really was a body out there. When I drove by, I hadn't seen anything like an ambulance (or a hearse?) and they certainly weren't going to load a dead body up in the back of a squad car.

I had seen dead bodies before, of course. I had been there—the only one there—when Gramma died, though I still managed to sleep through the precise moment when she went.

She hadn't stirred or spoken for the eleven previous hours, but I still couldn't help but wonder if she had wanted to say something in those last few seconds when I had fallen down on the job. The girl in the forest had not died alone. Someone knew her last words and the look in her eyes when she went. That was a kind of vigil of its own, but that someone would surely never tell a soul. It seemed awfully unfair, all these girls out there with no one to speak for them, and with the rest of us—with me—so close by. I wondered if she had looked my way while it was happening. I wondered if she saw the yellow lights from the kitchen and imagined that someone might save her.

I took the flashlight from its place next to the back door and slipped on Gramma's rubber work boots, heading across the side-lawn toward the forest.

. . .

I walked in the general direction of the police cars I had seen, wondering if they had strung up that caution tape or anything like that. I'd seen that once before, wrapped around a burnt-out meth trailer like the worst Christmas ribbon imaginable.

I heard the sound—a crackling of larger branches that had to have been broken by a creature with some weight to it—before I saw the blaze from a flashlight.

Whoever was wielding it was holding it directly at eye-level. I automatically swung my own light up to where I imagined his or her face to be.

"Aw, fuck!" I heard and their flashlight dipped,

allowing me to blink the bright coronas from my eyes.

When my vision cleared, I could see that it was a man about three feet away in a Sheriff's department uniform. The blueish beam of the flashlight rendered the face above it a bit ghoulish, but I recognized it all the same: Tracey Finnerman. He was one of Devon's friends—his best friend, really—and like Devon, he was a few years older than me. Also like Devon, he was a bit of an ass.

Unlike Devon, he'd actually managed to get his shit together after high school, though everybody knew that the only reason he got in at the Sheriff's office was because his mom had been a police dispatcher for decades and nobody wanted to piss her off.

"Frannie? What the hell are you doing out here?"

" . . . mushroom'n." I stared down at the ground between us as though scouring it for unexpected fungi.

"At three in the morning?" A little bit of the cop's neutral, interrogative lilt crept into Tracey's voice.

"Gramma always told me that was the best time."

Tracey trained his flashlight on my face again so I could no longer see his. I had no idea if he was buying any of this, but it was hardly illegal to go wandering around in the woods at night. Ill-advised, sure, but not against the law.

"You can't be out here right now," Tracey pronounced finally, lowering the flashlight again.

"Well, now that you've blinded me, I'll just stumble homewards."

"Oh shit! Sorry, Frannie." Instantly, he was the Tracey I remembered from high school, trying awkwardly to force the flashlight back into his belt. Gramma used to say that when God was handing out elbows, Tracey went back for seconds. "Here, I'll help you," he reached forward and grabbed my arm with a degree of force he probably didn't intend, sending me stumbling toward him.

"Jesus, Tracey, pull my arm out of the socket, why don't you?"

"Shit," he said again, but very soft this time, like

someone who had grown accustomed to small personal failures. "Sorry."

"I'm fine. I don't need an escort and you can't just walk away from a crime scene anyway."

In the dim light from his lowered flashlight, I could see his brows screw up in confusion. "How did you know it was a crime scene?"

"Cops out in the middle of the woods on a school night? It's either a crime scene or a real inconvenient doughnut sale."

* * *

"You found another body, didn't you?" I asked, as we cleared the trees and headed into the half-grown stalks of corn.

"Frannie, you know I can't say anything about open investigations."

"So, whatever's in the woods is part of an open investigation?" In Our Lady that pretty much just meant the dead women.

"Frannie! Stop fishing!"

"Hey, this is a public safety concern. If I need to curtail my mushroom'n activities for the time being, I'd prefer to know sooner rather than later."

Tracey sighed. "First of all, there's never a good time to go wandering in the forest after dark. Secondly, you aren't the kind of girl this guy is after. So don't worry about it."

"What kind of girls are those?"

"You know," he said wearily, "not local girls. The kind that are passing through."

It was strange to admit that Tracey Finnerman was right about something but I was a local girl, as local as it got. I wasn't ever going anywhere else.

"And what are y'all going to do about it?"

We came to the edge of the field, a little dip in the dirt before it bled into my patchy, unkempt lawn.

"Oh, the usual. Bend over and take it from the state police when they come out."

Despite all the bodies turning up in Our Lady, the dead girls had never been a local case. The state was handling it now, though there were rumblings about the feds getting involved.

"Did she look familiar?"

"Huh?" Tracey asked.

"The woman. In the woods. Did she look like someone you might have seen around?"

Tracey looked at me like I'd just told an off-color joke. "Uh . . . no. No, she didn't look like anybody."

We were silent then until we drew up to the yellow glow of my back-porch.

"You, uh, hear much from your brother these days?" Tracey asked suddenly, as I moved to climb the steps.

"Nope," I said. I hadn't seen Devon since I caught him swiping Gramma's liquid morphine. I don't know if he was taking it himself or selling it (and I wasn't sure which was worse, honestly) but I told him that he had to leave and he couldn't come back until he got his shit together. I took from his long silence that his shit was still well-dispersed.

"That's a shame," Tracey awkwardly opined.

I just shrugged and climbed the rest of the steps to the screen door.

"I could, uh, stay," Tracey offered, wincing as though the words had cut him on their way out of his mouth.

My hand hovered over the door latch while I emitted a flat, consistent "uhhhhhhh" tone, like a skeptical alarm clock.

"Outside, I mean. I could stay out-side . . . and . . . protect you. Keep watch, that sort of thing."

He meant well. He meant to make me feel safe. Unfortunately, few things made me feel less safe than the thought of Tracey Barney Fife-ing his way around my house in the dark. I wouldn't sleep all night, wor-rying he was going to step in a gopher hole and snap his ankle.

"Nah, Tracey," I said, as gently as I could manage. "It's like you said, I don't got anything to worry about. Besides, I still have Gramma's .22"

Tracey laughed like he was still experimenting with

the concept of mirth. "Anything under a .38 is just about useless against an assailant, though."

"Thanks for the tip, Officer Finnerman."

Tracey shifted his weight awkwardly, reaching up as if to doff his hat before thinking better of it. I opened the screen door and stepped up into the kitchen. It felt weird, closing the door with him just standing there looking at me but I wasn't sure what else I could do.

In the kitchen, I crossed over to the window and, sure enough, he was still standing there with no indication that he intended to move.

"*Goodnight*, Tracey!" I called through the window glass, giving him a wave.

"Uh, goodnight!" he answered back, his voice muffled and far away.

"You get you some sleep," I added before turning out the light and heading back toward my sofa. It was tomorrow already and the both of us were just working stiffs after all.

The diner's clientele could be sorted into three groups. There were the locals, who came in all the time, the truckers, who stopped by when their runs took them through this part of the country, and there were the strangers who were usually lost on their way to somewhere better. On Thirsty Thursdays, all three categories were well-represented.

Technically, The Our Lady Diner wasn't zoned for alcohol but Jace Coolidge, who owned the diner and the expanded convenience store connected to it, was pretty lax about letting people buy booze at the store and bring it over.

"Hey girl." A man with a large pot-belly and a backwards trucker cap grinned at me from a counter stool.

"Hey Doug," I answered, making my way behind the counter and retrieving my apron. Doug was a trucker. He and his wife Kathleen came through every few months with their ancient chocolate lab, the only dog that Jace allowed in the diner.

"How are you all doing?"

"Oh, pretty good. Stopped in St. Louis, saw that big arch." His face wrinkled, taking on a worried, fatherly cast. "Glad to see you're doing fine. I don't like you living all alone like you do with all this crap going on." I guess news of the new girl in the forest had gotten around.

"I do all right," I assured him. "I can take care of myself.

Doug gave a big, jolly Santa Claus laugh. "I bet you can! They grow 'em tough out here, huh?"

"Sure do," I smiled, refilling his coffee. I stirred in special honey that I reserved for my favorite customers and gave him a dollop of real whipped cream.

"You're a treasure," he said when I handed it to him.

Just then, Daisy burst out from the back with three plates on each arm. "Thank God!" she exclaimed, sliding past me to deliver her burdens at various tables.

"Christine skipped out at five." Daisy came back around the counter and grabbed the coffee pot with a shaky hand.

"What? Why?"

"Said she had to go buy a lotto ticket." Daisy looked at Doug's full cup in consternation and then glanced around, wondering what she was now to do with the pot of coffee in her hand. I removed it gently.

"So you've been alone for two hours?" Christine was the sweetest woman you could imagine but she was a born flake. She probably got some tip—whether it was from a TV preacher, her psychic, or a goddamned fortune cookie—and had to run off right away to play her magic numbers.

Daisy nodded, her eyes huge. Daisy was fifteen and had only been working at the diner for a little more than a month. Her face was bright red from the heat of the kitchen, and yellow hair was escaping her ponytail, plastered to her face and neck with sweat. The front of her apron and even her uniform shirt, was stained and caked with spilled food.

"Why didn't you just call me?"

"I didn't have time!" Daisy wailed. "It's been packed since she left!"

"Alright, alright." I gave her shoulder a squeeze. "Go in the back and take your break. Pee, check your phone, change your apron for fuck's sake, and then get back out here, it's gonna be a long night."

"Thank you, Frannie!" she leaned forward and kissed me on the cheek, a little girl's gesture of thanks.

"Poor kid," Doug chuckled.

"Yeah, Jace really oughta hire another waitress. Cheaper to work us to death, though."

"Are you guys hiring?" On the stool next to Doug, Shayna was being so quiet I hadn't noticed her. Shayna was something between a trucker and a stranger, a traveling girl who had been hanging around Our Lady for a while now. She panhandled out by the forty-six exit and usually only got enough for a sandwich or a slice of pie, if that. I would always let her linger if I was on shift. I thought it was better, her dozing in the booth or scribbling something in her sketchpad here in the warm, fluorescent safety of the diner.

"I wish," I sighed. "Why, you wanna put in your application?"

Shayna shrugged.

"You could draw little pictures on the menus," I teased. Shayna told me once that she was on her way to San Francisco where she had the kind of fun aunt who made jewelry and baked pot cookies. Shayna was gonna sell her art out there and go to the beach every day. "What are you working on?" I asked. She flipped her pad toward me so I could see a remarkably lifelike sketch of King. Underneath Doug's seat, King himself slapped his tail against the counter in approval.

After Daisy came back from her break (hair smoothed and apron replaced) the night settled into the typical trajectory of a Thirsty Thursday. It was okay until about ten-thirty. By then, folks who liked to drink had been doing it for a few hours and a lot of the families and kids had already eaten dinner and left.

I always tried to predict which of the customers were most likely to become the flashpoint of a *situation* and, this particular night, my money was on Ray Keene and his girlfriend Corey Wilde. Ray Keene was an oddball in more ways than one. He was a trucker and he didn't live in Our Lady but he spent a lot of time here. He usually shacked up with Corey, who *was* local. I thought he also had some family around here, cousins or something, and he'd been around for almost a decade. He was a fixture of the town, like the potholes and the occasional leaks of sewage into the water supply.

Corey, I knew personally. She wasn't exactly one of Devon's friends but she was in his orbit. She used to wear a safety pin in her nose and had once nearly beaten a girl to death on school property. The other girl had called her a "trailer-trash skank." The beating—along with a few other incidents—led to Corey dropping out in her senior year.

I didn't know exactly what she did for money but it was probably wasn't, as Gramma would have said, "a daylight job." I figured that's how she met Ray, who was a good fifteen years older than her and a spectacular asshole to boot.

They came in on Thursdays pretty often and, like tonight, they were usually loaded (if not worse) before they arrived. I took the table automatically—this was way beyond Daisy's paygrade.

"Hi folks!" I chirruped at them, pretending not to notice how Corey's head kept sagging and rolling on her neck or how Ray was fiddling with the button on her jeans. "What can I get for you?"

Ray had his usual—burger and fries—while Corey mumbled something that sounded like "lasagna," which we didn't serve. Ray had a large bottle of generic vodka nestled against his side, half-empty.

"It's our anniversary," he told me, beaming. Corey made a motion that might have been a nod or might have just been her falling asleep.

"Jesus tap-dancing Christ," I muttered to Daisy as I circled around the counter. "They are a walking anti-drug PSA." Daisy's eyes got big as she peered around me to gawk. Ray was whispering something in Corey's ear while she just stared ahead, her eyes shiny and uncomprehending.

"She's bruised up," Daisy observed. "Around her neck, like someone's been choking her."

Daisy had a good eye. Corey had tried to powder over it with makeup, but there were indeed dark splotches just under her jawline. Everyone who knew her knew that Ray beat her. One time, he broke her pelvis. She hadn't even tried to make up a story about how that happened.

"Yup," I said, "he's a real prince."

"But she's so young. She could go somewhere else, do anything," Daisy observed.

I was surprised to hear that Daisy thought of Corey as "young." She was twenty-one, three years older than me. "Some people get stuck early in life," I told Daisy.

· · ·

Around twelve-thirty, a couple of tourists from Los Angeles came in. The woman had long, flawlessly tousled hair and was wearing a shirt made out of what appeared to be tatted lace. Her male companion had his phone out and didn't seem to notice the way that Ray Keene was leering at the woman.

Corey did, though, and she gave Ray a venomous look as she got up to use the bathroom. I kept one eye on the door—she was in there an awful long time and I had a feeling that, one way or another, she was gonna make a mess I'd have to clean up.

The LA guy ordered a large black coffee and the woman got a milkshake and the two of them settled in at the bar next to Shayna. "Take care of them," I told Daisy, "and try to hurry them along if you can."

"No problem," Daisy said. "Actually, though, can I ask a favor?"

"What's up?"

"Would you take booth three?"

I glanced over to the booth in question. It was a high school kid about Daisy's age but, unlike the others, he was all alone. "Why? He try something?" Jace was an ass almost all the time but he would have our backs if we kicked out someone for getting handsy.

"No, no, no!" she said immediately. "He's just someone I know from school and I don't . . . like him, I guess. Matty Sands. He's a weird kid."

I chuckled. I could remember many an awkward, forced interaction with classmates I despised back when I was still in high school. Thankfully, most of the people in my class had left town after graduation. "Okay, I'll see to the creeper in the booth and Sid and Nancy over there, you keep an eye on the counter and we might just make it through this night."

Over at the booth, I took a closer look at Daisy's nemesis. He was thin and curly-headed with a patchy teenager beard and he had a bottle of something buried in a brown paper bag from the convenience store.

His eyes were slightly glassy and I thought at first that he was wasted because I had to ask him a few times what he wanted. Then I realized he wasn't drunk, he was just staring at the counter. Staring specifically at the woman from LA like he was trying to undo her top with the power of his mind.

"You gonna order?" I asked loudly.

"Pie." He spit the word like it was a racial slur. I inched myself over until I was blocking his view of the counter.

"Sure, we've got strawberry-rhubarb, cherry, marionberry, banana cream, and chocolate silk."

The kid grimaced, clearly annoyed that I was interrupting his ogling session but unwilling to sacrifice his dignity by shifting to look around me. "Chocolate. With whipped cream," he snapped and I decided that he was going to get the shitty Cool-Whip and not the nice stuff.

"I can see why you're not a fan," I told Daisy when I returned to the counter to cut his slice of chocolate pie.

Daisy suppressed a small shudder. "That whole family is fucked—excuse me—*messed* up."

I slopped an ugly dollop of Cool-Whip on the pie and grinned at Daisy. "Last chance to spit on it before I go." Daisy looked scandalized and I laughed. "Relax! I wouldn't really do that. If I did, Ray Keene's burger would be more spit than cow."

Speaking of Ray Keene, I noticed as I walked the pie over that he wasn't in his booth anymore. Corey had finally returned, her eyes fever-bright and her fingers moving restless against the formica, tapping out a code only she understood. Like Matty, she was staring at the LA woman, watching every small movement the other woman made.

That was ominous, sure, but it was still Ray's absence that worried me more. "You see where Ray went to?" I asked Daisy as I passed. She pointed out the big windows where Ray was smoking beside another, smaller figure. Shayna. There was something about the sight of the two of them standing there, just shadows in the glow of the exterior lights, that I did not like.

I pushed out the front doors and called out to Shayna. She had her hood pulled over her face and Ray stood next to her with his wallet in his hand and I liked *that* even less than seeing them smoking together.

"Shayna," I said, "I have the last piece of chocolate silk pie going begging if you want it."

She nodded and stubbed out her cigarette, practically hopping back over to me and the open door.

As I ushered her inside I could feel someone looking at me and I wasn't at all surprised to look up and see Ray Keene's smug stare. He smiled at me—and it wasn't very customer-friendly, but I didn't smile back.

I tried to back into the restaurant but ran immediately into Shayna who was standing in the doorway, staring.

Corey, looking more animated than she had all evening, was standing (well, swaying) at the edge of her booth venting a stream of mostly-coherent invective at the girl from LA. The girl was right up in Corey's face, wagging her finger angrily. For a moment, I wondered what would happen if Corey stretched her neck out like a vicious dog and bit that finger off in one short snap.

Instead, Corey reared back and gave the LA girl an almighty shove, sending her stumbling into the counter. The movement was like lighting a match in a mine full of flammable gas: everything exploded at once.

The girl from LA staggered upright while her companion reached out a hand either to steady her or hold her back from Corey who advanced upon the two of them. "Just try something, bitch!" Corey spit and the girl from LA made a noise like an outraged animal. Matty Sands, who was also standing up for some reason, slunk back along the wall toward the men's room.

The bell over the door jangled and Ray Keene burst in. "She hurt you?" he demanded, striding over to Corey and taking her arm in a bruising grip.

"Tried." Corey hocked what was surely a horrifying loogie at the girl from LA.

"What the fuck are you talking about?" the LA girl screamed, ducking out of the way of the phlegm-missile. "You attacked me, you psycho!"

"Come in here with your ass hanging out of your shorts, thinking you're so much better than us dirty hicks . . ."

"That little shit grabbed my ass!" the girl from LA insisted, her voice going high with disbelief.

Everyone looked over then at Matty, who had frozen, just inches from the men's room door.

"I didn't," he mumbled, all deer-in-the-headlights.

"He didn't!" Corey crowed. "Every man in the world ain't trying to fuck you!"

The LA girl gave her a bitter look. "What is *wrong* with you?"

Corey ripped her arm out of Ray's grip and launched herself at the LA girl, who threw her arms up defensively, scratching at any part of Corey she could reach.

"Hey! Hey! Hey," I cried as Ray Keene charged in, grabbing the LA girl by the arm the same way as he had done with Corey. For just a second, he stared at her before giving her a slap that made her cry out and sag in his grip.

"Get your hands off her!" I screamed at Ray who lifted both of his hands in the air like I had a gun on him. The LA girl touched her nose, which was dribbling blood.

"I slipped," he smirked, and I felt a dangerous kind of rage. The kind of anger that made me sincerely wish I *did* have a gun to put on him.

"You didn't *slip*, you—" I started.

Then, the bell over the door jangled once again. I had never in my life been so happy to see Tracey Finnerman's confused face.

It wasn't unusual for some deputies to swing by the diner, especially on Thursdays. They had to eat just like anyone else and sometimes them just putting in an appearance was enough to defuse rough situations.

"Thank God," I muttered, walking over to Tracey and his partner, Stuart Matheson. Stuart was an older fella and I knew him from way back; he used to chase Devon (and sometimes Tracey) all over the county.

"What the hell's going on here, Frannie?" Stuart asked.

"I was hoping that was something you could sort out."

"Actually, I just wanted a burger," Tracey admitted.

"You deal with this and I'll give you one on the house."

Stuart strode forward. "Sit your asses down," he said, pushing Ray Keene and the man from LA into opposing booths. He paused and looked at the woman from LA and winced at her reddened nose. "Get her a cold washcloth or something," he told Daisy, who ran into the back obediently.

"Okay," Tracey said, "we're gonna talk one at a time and no interrupting. It's kindergarten rules." He pointed at the girl from LA. "You, go. Start at the beginning."

"I went to the bathroom," the woman said, gratefully taking a damp washcloth from Daisy and dabbing it against her nose. "And on my way back, that kid in the corner tries to feel me up. I call him on it and the *Cops* reject over there"—she gestured at Corey who threw up both middle fingers—"got up in my face. She's the one who put her hands on me. I did nothing but defend myself."

Corey snorted.

"And?" Tracey said, turning to her. "Any truth in that?"

"*Princess* decided she wasn't getting enough attention," Corey sneered. "So she tried to start shit, make sure everybody was looking at her again. I gave her what she wanted."

"You use any narcotics tonight, Corey?" Tracey asked, though he must surely have known the answer.

Corey must have thought so too, because she just rolled her eyes.

"If I were to search you now, am I gonna find something I wouldn't like?"

Corey gave him what must have been her best sultry look. Even with her smeared makeup, the now-clearly visible bruises on her neck and the junkie hollows in her cheeks, I could still see some of that punk-slut charm she had back when she ran with Devon and Tracey and all the rest of them. "Depends on how *extensive* that search is gonna be." She grinned at him, red showing in between her teeth.

Tracey sighed. "Corey, you need another charge like you need a hole in the head."

"I want to press charges," the girl from LA insisted. Alone in his booth, Ray Keene smiled at nothing in particular. Tracey and Stuart exchanged a quick look and Tracey gestured to me.

"Why don't you get her cleaned up while we deal with this, okay?"

I nodded and led the girl from LA to the private bathroom in the back that the staff used.

"Yikes," she said when saw her face in the mirror, and I had to agree. The side of her face where Ray had slapped her was already puffing up and she was definitely going to have a bruise under that eye. "Fucking lunatic," she muttered, gingerly wiping away the congealed blood underneath her nose.

"He is that." I unrolled a healthy portion of TP and handed it to her.

"He does this kind of thing a lot?" she asked, shocked.

"Not this exactly. But dumb shit." This was the first time I'd really ever seen Ray at "Peak Ray," but I'd heard the same stories everyone else had. How he beat the shit out of a dude for "stealing" his car after he got too plastered to find it, how he caused the fire that burned down Corey's mother's trailer by trying to cook meth on his own, how his trucks always came in mysteriously light and he always had a little extra cash after to throw around after he finished a run. "Every town has one, I suppose."

The girl from LA snorted. "God, I hope not."

Tracey was waiting for us when we got out of the bathroom. "Oh, well, that's not too bad," he said with too much forced cheer in his voice. The woman from LA looked at him like he was an idiot.

"I'm pressing charges," she said, speaking slowly and clearly. "I'll sue, do whatever I have to."

Tracey cocked his head to one side. "But *will* you? Will you stick around here in Our Lady for the months—possibly years—it's going to take to push this case through our over-burdened county court system? And that's presuming that we're talking about a best case scenario here where everyone in the diner is willing to testify to your version of events—"

"My *version?*"

"And," Tracey continued loudly, "I can tell you right now that this is not a best case scenario. Plus, even if you did have a best case scenario—which, again, I must stress this is *not*—there's absolutely no guarantee that Ray would even show in court. He's a long-haul trucker, he travels for a living and Corey is . . . well, you've met her. Does she strike you as the type to hew closely to the letter of the law?"

The woman from LA said nothing; her face was stormy and her flesh swollen but I could tell that she had no counter for Tracey's argument. He reached out and patted her on the shoulder awkwardly.

"How about you and your husband get back on the road and go where you're going and you have a wonderful time there and you forget all about this unpleasantness? Frannie'll even comp your meal, so it'll be like you were never here at all."

"You're telling me that a dude *slapped me in the fucking face* in front of five other people and my only restitution is a gas station milkshake?"

I tried not to bristle at her description of the diner as a "gas station."

Tracey smiled. "Better than a slap in the face and *no* milkshake," he said.

• • •

"C'mon," the LA woman said, stalking back into the restaurant and grabbing her man by the collar. "Let's get out of this backwoods, pig-fucking, piece of shit town." She glared around the room at all of us as she said, daring us to try something. No one did. Even

Corey just watched quietly as they left, slamming the door.

"Miss Wilde, why don't you come down to the station for the night? Get you sorted and have our nurse look at you," Stuart suggested to Corey, who was limp and listless again.

Tracey looked at me. "Guess it'll be a raincheck on that burger."

"I guess so," I said, watching as Stuart helped Corey to her feet, holding on to her elbow like a boy guiding his drunk prom date into a limo.

"Am I free to go then?" Ray asked, looking between Tracey and Stuart.

Tracey stared back at him, something unreadable in his face. "Yeah." He sounded deflated. "You're free to go."

Ray followed Stuart and Corey out the door. "I'll pick you up in the morning, baby," I heard him say as they vanished into the cool dark of the parking lot.

Tracey lingered in the doorway, like I was gonna say something to him.

"I think I'm gonna close up now," I said pointedly and Tracey shook his head like a dog shaking off water.

"Right, sure. Okay. I'll . . . go, then," he opened the door and got halfway out before stopping again. "I'm serious about that raincheck," he said.

I gave him a mock-salute. "Yes, Officer Finnerman."

He chuckled and backed out the door.

· · ·

I sent Daisy home early—as a minor, she wasn't supposed to work past midnight anyway. I told Joanne and Parker in the kitchen they could go home too. We'd all had about enough for one night.

And then I was alone.

That was actually how I liked the diner best, in those solitary moments before or after a shift. The quiet and the stillness, the emptiness. When we were getting toward the end with Gramma, those times felt like the only real silence I got.

It took about an hour to complete the closing checklist solo and I was finishing up the mopping in the front of the diner when I saw something move in my peripheral vision. I looked out the big front windows and saw nothing but darkness. We used to have lights, streetlamp-style out in the middle of the parking lot, but one by one, the bulbs either burned out or got broken and Jace was too cheap to replace them.

I had a sense of size and movement, like someone had just glided past the door in a car. It could have been a tourist trying get back on the highway or it could have been someone heading for the pumps in the convenience store's parking lot.

But without their lights on?

I finished mopping, trying to move as normally as possible, turned off all the lights both interior and exterior, like I was going to leave for the night. Then

I crept, ducking low to stay under the edge of the window, back up to the front of the restaurant.

With all the lights out I had a reasonably good view of the parking lot, but there was nothing. Just darkness and stillness and more of that silence that, just a few hours ago, I would have said I appreciated. It was stupid, me cowering in front of the window all paranoid and jumpy. I could have said it was the fight that had me so shook but fights in the diner were nothing new.

Nevertheless, I couldn't stop staring out at that barren parking lot, the street in front of it just as empty. All that blank space and still I could not shake the feeling that I was not alone.

Forest Interlude

2

I'm Death I come to take the soul

Leave the body and leave it cold

To draw up the flesh off of the frame

Dirt and worm both have a claim

  —*O Death, Traditional*

I tried to bury my body the next day.

It was easier for me to keep track of the days but I had trouble with smaller chunks of time. Minutes got away from me. Hours slipped by while I wasn't looking. It was like time had gotten light and fragile, like dandelion fluff, and it would only stay while I was motionless. The minute I moved or directed my attention elsewhere, it flew away and vanished into the air.

Everything suddenly took so much energy, so much concentration. It had seemed so easy when I watched him do it, molding and propping me up like one of those big dolls they give to little girls. Remember those? The ones that are made to order so you can get the same height, same hair, same eyes, as a living girl? I never had one of those myself, though I remember seeing the commercials on the TV and feeling that unfulfilled ache of little-kid greed. It's easy when you're little to convince your-self that, with the right supplies, you can transform yourself into the smiling girl on the TV with her clean, carefully curated bedroom and all her laugh-ing friends.

Now I had a double of my very own but I couldn't do anything to her. I couldn't lift her arms or move her legs or drag her away from her tree. I couldn't even braid her hair, though it did flutter slightly when I tried to touch it, like a very gentle wind was playing with it.

The way her hair moved gave me an idea and I

turned my attention to the fallen leaves and the twigs and the loose dirt around the dead me, pushing them up toward my feet, my legs, until I could build the debris into little piles all around my body. It was slow going, sure, but it was steady and time was on my side. It was just about the only thing that was.

Every once in a while, though, the real wind would move through the trees from the opposite direction and scatter my pathetic little shroud. After the fifth or sixth time this happened, I gave up.

.   .   .

I had an idea that if I could just cover my body, protect it a little bit from the elements, then it might let me go away.

I figured I still owed my body. It had protected and encased me and it was my job to protect it and preserve it in return. I had clearly screwed up my half of the bargain but my body was holding me to it anyway. I had no reason to believe this, but it *felt* true.

I still tried to get away, though. Sometimes I went toward a place where the trees seemed a little thinner or headed in a direction that I hadn't been before. Sometimes I went down the exact same path I'd tried more times than I could count because sometimes it was different and I had no idea why.

At first I thought it was just me, that I was getting lost. Every goddamned pine tree looks pretty much like every other goddamned pine tree after all, but then I started to pick out certain features that clustered together. The half-rotted pine whose upturned branches looked like a hand grabbing at the sky next to a huge boulder furred with green moss, the fast-moving river that swelled in some places and slowed to a trickle in others, the big arcing trees that made a weird little cave, like a fort for some kid. I saw those things again and again but they never seemed to show up in the exact same configuration and sometimes they would be slightly changed—a live tree where I knew a dead one had been, a barren riverbed where water was supposed to be. Once, I saw the grasping pine all on fire, orange arcing up toward the sky. And then it was back again, dry and curled but unburnt.

And no matter how far I went or in what direction, I always came back to myself. I could never be exactly sure when it would happen. Sometimes the forest would let me go for what could have been days—months, I guess—until it felt like I had to have crossed into a different state. Other times, I would just go a few feet before I turned around to find myself back where I started. It was like I was on one of those extra-long retractable leashes people get for their dogs. The lead will just keep spooling out on those until maybe the dog thinks he's free, but inevitably, the owner is gonna pull him up short and remind him of how things really are.

It seemed too random to be malicious, though it certainly sometimes felt that way. It's just that I would get so *close* sometimes; I would be sure that

I could hear the cars on the freeway and then I'd clear a stand of trees or come around the edge of a rock and there I would be again, alone with myself. Once, I crawled what felt like forever through a low, thorny bush bristling with unripe berries and, when I came out the other side, I was inches away from my own dead face, turned ever upwards and away from me.

. . .

I could not forget that I was dead. I was not *allowed* to forget, though there was so much else that I couldn't remember anymore. I thought my name had started with an M (Mary? Martha? Mady? Monica?), I thought I might have had a sister, maybe more than one. I couldn't even clearly recall the face of the man who murdered me but I knew at all times that I had, in fact, been killed.

I hadn't felt it—or I didn't remember feeling it—when he did those things to me and left me there but I had a . . . knowledge that was at least partly physical or sensory, that I was decaying.

The bugs liked the parts of me that were close and wet; the parts that were in contact with the dirt were the best. They were the first things to show up, coming on so quickly it was alarming. It was like deciding to move out of an apartment and waking up the next morning to find someone already in your kitchen, unpacking all their shit.

The bugs felt to me like anxiety, like something moving fast and industrious but packed tight together. It felt almost . . . buzzy, like the pleasure-pain that pop made when you just let it sit on your tongue. I would do that when I was younger— take a big drink of pop and hold it in my mouth as long as I could stand it. I had the incredibly dumb idea that it was burning something away inside of me, that it was cleaning me the way a corrosive acid will make metal shine like new.

That's what it felt like, being consumed.

The larger a scavenger was the longer it waited

to come for me. Like any opportunists, they only wanted the softest, easiest parts of me—my nose and my mouth, my hands and feet, my privates and my throat—those places where he had already injured me and made it easier to tear my flesh away from itself.

The tearing didn't feel like pain. It wasn't hot or sharp or paralyzing the way I remember pain to be. It felt more like having something that was precious and important, something you wanted to carry with you all the time, and feeling that thing pulled out of your hands by someone bigger and stronger who didn't care anything about you.

But I didn't begrudge the critters their meal. They're just animals, after all.

I almost never saw the rotting that I knew I was doing. When the forest would lead me back to myself, I nearly always looked just as I had when he dragged me there and left me. Only every once in a while would I discover, instead, a putrefying thing, skin sinking into the spaces between all my bones. Once, I saw myself as nothing more than a collection of those bones, not even in the right shape either. The creatures of the forest had scattered me so completely that I had become just another part of the earth out there. My hair grew into the moss and grasses, my bones sank into the moist dirt until they were just winks of white, like hidden stones. Everything soft about me lived only in the bellies of the grubs and the worms.

I probably should have been glad that my body didn't look like that very often but I might have actually preferred that. Going from a dead thing down to bones was natural and it was something that had happened to every other living thing since the earth began. Whatever else she was, the girl who had been me with her face toward the clouds and her throat a collection of bruises, she was not natural.

3

I had a few options, none of them ideal. I could:

1: Stay right here. All the doors there were shut and locked, though that wouldn't exactly stop someone intent on getting at me. It would mean an uncomfortable few hours and Jace would likely be irritated when he came in tomorrow and found one of his waitresses curled up like a bum in one of his booths. The biggest thing, though, was my own stubborn resistance to the mental image of me crouching there all night like some scared kid.

So, option number 2: I could call someone to pick me up. Except that I had no idea who that someone would be. Gramma was gone now and Devon too, they were all the real family I had in the world. If I called Jace, I'd probably just get an earfull about waking him in the middle of the night. Daisy didn't even have her driver's license and Christine had two kids in bed. She wasn't gonna want to get up and go run over to the diner to pick up her paranoid co-worker at three AM.

That left me with just one option: I could just suck it up and be an adult. I would walk across the parking lot at my place of work where I had walked a million times before and I would get in my car and drive myself home, just like any other night. And if anyone tried anything, I'd fuck them up.

Admittedly, I had no idea *how* I was going to fuck them up but I wasn't going to live my life jumping at shadows, terrified of . . . of what? Of bodies in the woods? Of a man who thought so little of this place and those women that he left them out to rot? No, that wasn't how I lived. Not in my own town.

Still, I stopped by the dish drainer on my way out the back and grabbed a thin, wicked fish knife on my way out.

I held it slightly out in front of myself as I stepped out into the parking lot, letting the moonlight catch on it and glitter. I forced myself to walk at a normal pace, looking from side to side as I crossed the parking lot to my car.

I was so focused on looking out for approaching vehicles that I almost stepped over the book. It was lying open on the pavement in front of my driver's side door. I recognized it, even in the dim moonlight—Shayna's sketchbook, each page tight with doodles and sketches and intricate drawings, no space wasted. I recognized thumbnail portraits of diner regulars and nature drawings of what looked like locations in the state forest.

Shayna didn't have much in the world, not even a big bag like some traveling kids I saw. She had a little purse, her giant jacket, and this sketchpad. I never saw her without those things and I had a low, ugly feeling in my stomach that told me she would not have abandoned this in a parking lot. And, if she had forgotten it, I felt like she surely would have returned for it.

If she *could* return.

I had assumed that Shayna had left the diner on foot. I knew she stayed in town sometimes, either at the Presbyterian church or with kind people who offered her a bed for a day or two. Did someone make her that kind of offer tonight? Did she drop her pad out of a car?

An image floated up in my mind of Ray Keene with his wallet out and Shayna with a borrowed cigarette in her hand. Again, I felt that formless fear and distrust. A . . . *wrongness*, I supposed.

I flicked on my headlights and pulled out of the parking lot, heading for the highway forty-six exit. Shayna had mentioned before that she "had a place" out there for those nights when she couldn't find a bed in town.

The exit was quiet and barren. Distantly, trucks

were roaring along on the highway. I pulled over alongside the turn lane and stepped out of the car, loose gravel and old, crumbled windshield glass crunching under my feet. There was a little gully next to the big Our Lady sign (the one with "of the River's Mouth" crammed in tiny print at the bottom) and I saw that Shayna had strung up a blue plastic tarp between a few scraggly trees. There was a swept-clean place underneath it where someone small might have curled up out of the weather. There was a space for her, an absence where she should have been, but no Shayna. She was gone.

·   ·   ·

After a solid two minutes of knocking, a weary woman with a red braid and one of those long, old-lady house dresses appeared at the door of the little ranch-style house. "Frannie?" she squinted at me.

"Hey Mrs. Finnerman," I said, a little sheepishly.

"Sorry to wake you up but I really need to talk to Tracey. It's an emergency."

Her eyes widened in alarm. "Oh shit," she said, "you're pregnant."

I backed up automatically. "What? No. No! I'm not pregnant and this is a . . . crime emergency."

Eileen Finnerman pressed her hand over her heart. "Jesus, girl. Don't scare me like that."

"I'm . . . sorry?" I offered and Eileen gestured for me to come inside.

"Wait here," she told me, "I'll get him up."

I paced nervously between the sofa and the coffee table while the Finnermans' cat gave me a hostile stare. Finally, Tracey ambled down the stairs wearing the white t-shirt all the deputies had to wear under their uniforms and a pair of boxer briefs.

"Dammit, Tracey," I scolded, "put some pants on."

He rubbed some sleep from his eyes. "You show up at my house at three in the morning, you get what you get."

"First of all, it's your mom's house. Second of all, Shayna is missing."

"Who the hell is Shayna?" He ambled past me to give the cat a scratch behind the ears before drifting toward the kitchen. "You want something to eat?"

"No, I don't want anything to eat. She's a girl who comes into the diner."

"Who?"

"Shayna!"

"Shayna who?"

"Shayna the girl who is missing!" I hissed, resisting the urge to yell and disturb Mrs. Finnerman all over again. Tracey emerged from the fridge with the remains of a chicken breast and sat down at the table, not bothering with a plate or a fork.

"Okay. I don't know any Shayna, what's her deal?"

"She's a traveler, hitching rides, you know. Probably what you'd call a . . . transient, I guess?" I reluctantly took a seat opposite him, watching as he methodically shoved chicken into his mouth.

"And you're sure she didn't just . . . transiate away?"

"That's not remotely close to being a word and no. Not in the middle of the night, not without saying goodbye to anyone."

"People surprise you," he said, his voice slightly thick with chicken particles. "Everyone thinks they know what the people they love would or wouldn't do but they don't, not really."

I dropped the sketchpad on the table. "This is just about everything Shayna had in the world. Her most prized possession and I found it laying on the ground by my car, like . . . "

Like someone wanted me to find it.

Tracey flipped idly through the pad, licking his fingers. "She's pretty talented." He closed the pad and looked at me. "Okay, so, what do you want me to do?"

"I want you to find her!"

"And how do you suppose I do that? You got any leads? Any idea where she went or who with?"

"I do," I hesitated slightly before plunging ahead. "I think she might be with Ray Keene."

"And what makes you think that?"

I struggled to put it into words. The helpless, sinking sensation I had when I looked at the two of them, the awful way Ray smiled at me. How easily, how calmly he'd slapped that woman. Corey had been unhinged, wild with anger and whatever was coursing through her veins, but Ray was cool and steady like an air traffic controller. He made a thoughtful, precise decision to smack that women in front of a room full of people because he believed, correctly, that none of us could stop him or punish him afterward.

"I've got a feeling," I said finally and even to me it sounded stupid.

"I'm sure you don't need me to remind you that Frannie DeMott's feelings are not admissible as evidence in a court of law?"

"I don't want you to put him on trial, just check up on him a little. Look, he just got into a physical altercation a few hours ago and he was visibly intoxicated. Some might even say it's your *job* to make sure he isn't raising hell somewhere else."

Tracey gave me a long look, finished his last bite of chicken and then chuckled. "Aw, shit, Frannie. I'd do anything for you."

"Except put on pants," I observed.

"Well, a man must have standards."

* * *

"Corey's still in the tank. Stuart always gets her cleaned up, feeds her breakfast." Tracey told me, settling himself in the passenger seat. "He does it as a favor to her mom. It sure as hell doesn't do anything for Corey. She gets out, hooks up with Ray again and . . . " he trailed off into a weary shrug.

"Fucking Ray Keene," I muttered, turning on to Park Street. I knew that Corey lived in the Ridgedale apartments and Ray squatted there with her.

"Why do you got such a hard-on for him all of a sudden anyway?" Tracey teased. "What'd he do to you?"

"You mean other than slap around a paying customer in my diner?"

I paused and allowed silence to fill the car for a moment before adding, "I just find it a little suspicious how another body turns up in the forest and he comes back into town and then Shayna goes missing. Seems like a lot of activity all at once, is all."

"That body in forest wasn't . . . " Tracey searched for the right words. " . . . fresh." He did not find the right words. "I saw it for myself. It had been there a while, maybe a year or more."

"Like I said, I'm not trying to charge him with anything, I'm just . . . I'm just worried about my friend."

Tracey smiled at me, less teasing and more fond. "Frannie DeMott, still momming folks."

"Well, someone had to look after you idiots," I

said, thinking unavoidably of the night of Devon and Tracey's graduation when they got rip-shit drunk and came stumbling in at four in the morning. I ran between the two of them, making sure Devon got all his vomit in the toilet and stitching up a dripping cut on Tracey's scalp close to his hairline.

I looked sidelong at him, looking sleepy in the passenger seat. You could still see the scar, which wasn't surprising, I think I used some of Gramma's regular sewing thread on him. I had to hide him all night and wait until Gramma went off to the social security office in the morning before I could sneak him out the back.

"Park right here," he said, pointing to a spot on the far end of the Ridgedale parking lot. "They're in unit four-oh-seven."

"Been here a few times, huh?"

"I could find this place blind-folded."

"His truck isn't here," I said, parking the car and opening my door.

Tracey climbed out of the passenger side,

stretching and sighing. "Maybe he went to party somewhere else?"

It was officially morning now and in the soft, golden light I could see that unit four-oh-seven had its front window open and there didn't appear to be anyone inside, just the hulking shapes of furniture in a darkened room.

"Let's go in," I said, mounting the stairs.

Tracey chased after me and took my arm. "What? Are you crazy? That's not what you said we were doing!"

"I said we were finding Ray. So, let's be really, really certain he's not in there."

"Frannie, I can't just break into someone's apartment."

"I don't think it's breaking in if you have probable cause to believe a crime is being committed inside. Like, say, holding a teenage girl against her will."

"For the last time, Frannie, watching a lot of *Law and Order* doesn't make you an actual lawyer."

I halted on the step and turned to look at him. He was about four inches taller than me; it had always made lecturing him a challenge. "Are you gonna arrest me?"

"Of course not!"

"Well, *I'm* going to get into that apartment and you can help, or you can stand here, or you can arrest me. Those are your options."

Tracey huffed a little sigh but allowed me to pull my arm out of his grasp. I tried the door handle first, just in case Ray and Corey were as dumb as they seemed but it was in fact locked. I fished my debit card out of my purse and started working it between the door jam and frame.

"Ugh." Tracey followed me to the door, scowling in disapproval. "You can't just stand here working the lock. You know this place is full of nosy old folks who wake up at four in the morning." As if to illustrate his point, the curtains flickered in the unit across the landing from four-oh-seven. I thought

I glimpsed a sour, toothless face but it vanished as soon as it appeared.

"If you've just gotta do this," Tracey continued, "there's an easier way."

He took me by the hand and led me around to the back of the unit where there was a large sliding glass door. "All the units have these and they're fucking security black-holes, ridiculously easy to crack. We're out here once a week at least because someone got their TV boosted."

As if to demonstrate, he took the doors handle and shimmied it up and down slightly before shoving it back as hard as he could. We stepped through into the kitchen and were immediately assaulted by a monstrous stink.

"Dishes," Tracey said, hand clapped over his nose. Indeed, the sink was full of dishes and takeout containers as well as several inches of foul, brownish water.

On the couch in the living room was a tangle of mismatched and cigarette-charred blankets. On the table in front of this nest were several small squares of tinfoil with little deposits of something black in the center. The TV was on, tuned to one of those QVC-type channels and the volume was turned way up. I moved almost automatically to turn it down—I couldn't hear myself think—but Tracey stopped me.

"Don't. Don't disturb anything."

Was he afraid of Ray Keene getting mad because someone turned off his stories or what?

There was only one bedroom, mostly taken up by an enormous water bed. All the sheets and blankets had been stripped from it and the mattress itself was only semi-full. There was a thin layer of water lying across the top of it and the wood of the frame was swollen.

There was no sign of anyone, no indication that anyone had been there for hours or even days, but I still couldn't bring myself to leave. I drifted over to a large chest of drawers. One of the smallest drawers at the top was mostly closed but there was a corner of paper sticking out. I pulled the drawer open to find a folded sheet of paper hastily shoved on top of a pile of men's socks and underwear.

As I unfolded it, I realized my hands were shaking. I recognized this paper, the delicate and heavily detailed sketch of King the chocolate lab. I had watched as Shayna put the finishing touches on it right there in front of me at the diner.

"Tracey!" I called out, my voice trembling uncontrollably.

"Look at this!" I brandished the paper at him so aggressively that he had to take both of my hands to steady me. "This is one of Shayna's drawings. Why would he have this, Tracey? Why would he have her drawing?"

Tracey's eyes were soft but his face showed no emotion. It was his cop face, I supposed. "Okay, okay, just relax Frannie," he said, low and calm. "We're not going to freak out now. There are a lot of reasons he could have that paper." He knit his fingers through my free hand, gave it a comforting squeeze. It didn't help.

"Yeah? Tell me a few."

But Tracey was looking past me, down at the still-opened drawer. He removed his hand from mine and reached out to pluck what appeared to be a small plastic baggie out of the drawer. It was full of old-fashioned Polaroids.

"Fuck," I breathed. "Is that one of the missing women?"

In the photos, a blonde woman stared dully at the camera, her face an awful ruin with one eye nearly swollen shut and her mouth slightly open, lips all puffed up with trauma.

Tracey shook his head. "No, I've seen these pictures before. This is Corey."

It was hard to recognize her without her heavy makeup, her carefully done hair and her habitual bullet-proof scowl. In these pictures, Corey looked as young as Daisy seemed to think she was. It also looked like she had taken them herself. In several of the shots, I could see her arm extended so that she could get a shot of the purple-black spread of bruising across her ribs or the long fingernail scratches on her forearm.

"I remember these," Tracey's voice sounded uncharacteristically vacant. "Around the time I joined the Sheriff's office, she came in with these. She wanted to press charges and she said this was her proof."

"We told her we probably couldn't do anything for her and she took her pictures and she left. That was around the time he broke her pelvis and I always wondered if . . ." He trailed off, staring hard at the open drawer.

"If Corey took these pictures, then what are they doing in Ray's underwear drawer?"

"Maybe he—" Tracey winced, "—*likes* them."

I dropped the photos as though they were covered in an invisible layer of slime. Tracey immediately stooped to pick them up, putting them back in their bag and tucking them into the drawer just as he had found them.

"C'mon Frannie," he said, not ungently. "There's nothing here for us."

. . .

"Frannie," Tracey lingered in the car when I dropped him in front of his house. "You have to promise me that you won't do anything like that again."

For him, I knew, the job was over. Ray and Corey were just a sad situation that no one could do anything about and maybe he could live with that but I couldn't. I nodded, though because I knew there was no other way that he would leave.

"Promise me," Tracey said again, like he didn't trust my nod.

"I *promise*," I said and, as I pulled away, I kept looking at my purse, thinking about the crumpled sketch of King I had secreted inside. Ray Keene thought he was invincible and untouchable. He thought he could just take every little thing he wanted. Well, not this time. Not this girl. Not without a fight.

Forest Interlude

3

My lips they are as cold as clay

My breath smells earthy strong

And if you kiss my cold, clay lips

Your days they won't be long

    —*The Unquiet Grave, Traditional*

People came into the forest sometimes. They were alive, I couldn't say exactly how I knew that but I did know.

I liked to follow them because the forest never seemed to change when they were there, the trees all stayed the same height, the grasses didn't grow or retreat, boulder fields didn't shift or crumble. It was like . . . having something to hold on to, at least for a little while. But they never stayed very long and when they left the confines of the forest, I could not go with them.

I tried a couple of times to say something to them, to touch them or make myself noticed somehow but there was no reaction. I wasn't sure what I'd do if they did see me. Show them my body, maybe? Ask them to take it away, I guess? Put it in some hallowed ground and hope that would let me rest. Sometimes, they came real close to where I was—to where my body was. Sometimes, they were so close that I could not imagine how they couldn't have seen me sitting there.

Once a woman even slumped down next to me to rest her legs. If she reached out just a few inches, she could have held my hand. I had been tempted, in that moment, to try to move my dead hand, to extend it out toward hers.

I think that's why I grabbed that little boy out of the water, just because of the way he looked right at me and it had been so long since anyone had *seen* me.

He was too young to be out in the woods on his

own, but I didn't figure that was any of my business. His mom would be along to grab him soon. Or maybe she wouldn't. Maybe he had the kind of mother who didn't notice when her kid went missing.

Faces were hard for me. I knew he had very curly hair, the way little kids sometimes have, before they grow out of it. I remember it was reddish-blonde and I remember thinking that his pants were strange—all buttons and no zippers.

The river was fat and lazy that day. The water looked sluggish from the top but I knew the river's channel went deep and the current was strong whenever there was water to fill it. The little boy didn't shout even when he went in. I think the fall and the cold water surprised him. He sucked at the surface of the river, fighting for air and his small body stiffened up strangely. And then he looked right at me.

Something about his face or the awkward way he was holding himself made me remember something from long ago, from when I was not too much bigger than him. It was another river, far away. I was wearing a bathing suit with yellow ruffles on it. I remember because I waded out into the water to a place where the river picked up the edge of my suit and I twirled it around like a party dress.

That river was fast and cold too, and the bottom was sheathed in thick red clay. It was slicker than concrete glazed in ice and I had to be so, so careful picking my way across. There was another child there too and I don't remember how or who it was—not even whether it was a boy or a girl—just the feeling of little hands clinging to my waist.

I remembered walking with the little one in my arms, the water pulling at me in this awful longing way as though my rightful place in the world was downstream, floating like a skin of frog eggs or pond froth.

The memory was so vivid that it was hard for me to tell exactly when I had gone into the river after the boy. This time, I didn't feel the cold and I didn't have to work hard to stay on my feet. Even grabbing his little body, which had seemed so impossible before, was simple. He was feather light.

It had not been easy in that other river of my memory, every step had been a queasy negotiation between the pressure from the river and my own balance. But it had made me feel strong when we made it to the other side. It made me feel brave and benevolent, having protected someone even smaller than myself.

The boy never said anything to me, just stared at me with huge eyes, both adoring and afraid. But I wouldn't have cared if he looked disgusted or terrified, so long as he was looking at me. I wanted to keep him forever, someone to see me and know that I was real.

I didn't figure myself for a particularly maternal person but I wrapped him up in my arms like he was my own baby and held him against me. I held him as long as the forest would let me.

4

"**Y**ou know, my psychic said there was going to be a *significant discovery* and that I was going to experience a windfall and those things *both happened,*" Christine half-whispered, like it was a deadly secret.

"How much did you win?" Daisy inquired politely.

"Seventy-five dollars!" Christine crowed and I ducked into the back so she wouldn't see my massive eye-roll.

"Every time one of those girls showed up in the woods, JoJo has seen it. Every time!"

It struck me that JoJo might be better served predicting when those girls were going to be murdered rather than when their nameless bodies would turn-up.

"Frannie," Daisy called out, "your boyfriend's here!"

For a moment, I thought she was talking about Doug or one of the other regulars, then I emerged from the back and saw Tracey, back in uniform. He gave me a little sarcastic wave. "I'm here for my Burger of Valor," he said.

"Is that the name we're going with?"

"I'd like it medium rare with both kinds of cheeses, the yellow and the white. And I'd like onion rings instead of fries. Oh, and don't put a toothpick through it, use one of those plastic swords that they put in cocktails."

I snorted. "Take a seat. We'll try to meet your exacting standards."

"Just don't forget about the onion rings, that's the most important part."

"Tracey," Christine said, leaning heavily on the counter, "why don't you guys ever go out and see JoJo Sands? She could tell you where to look for those dead girls."

"We're not exactly *looking* for dead girls, Christine," Tracey corrected. "In fact, I'd prefer to avoid them, if I can."

"Oh, you know what I mean."

Daisy rounded the counter with a half-eaten plate of hot roast beef sandwich. "Wait, your psychic is JoJo *Sands*? Matty Sands's sister?"

Christine shrugged. "I guess?"

"Huh." Daisy slid the plate back towards the kitchen. "Guess that explains it. I told you that whole family was messed up."

"You talking about the kid who was in here the other night?" I asked. The ass-grabber's sister was Christine's psychic friend? I suppose that was the peril of a truly small town: everybody was something to everyone else.

"Yeah. Matty Sands. I knew his sister had

problems but I didn't know she was all weird like that. I guess that's why Matty's so . . . "

"He's so *what*?"

"Just . . . how he is, I guess. Real dark."

"Like a goth or something?"

"No, not like he was wearing black all the time or putting on eyeliner or whatever. It's more like . . . " Daisy looked embarrassed even as she said it. "Like some sort of aura. Angriness or sadness." She snapped her fingers. "You know that little comics guy who has the dirt cloud around him all the time."

"Pigpen," I supplied immediately. "From *Peanuts*."

"Yeah, that guy. Matty's like that. Except it wasn't dirt it was just this . . . bad, low feeling that never went away. Been that way since we were little kids."

"Like he felt bad? Or he made other people feel bad?"

Daisy screwed up her mouth like I'd wafted rotten food underneath her nose. "Both? I guess?"

"Every time," Christine was saying to Tracey again. "Every single time one of those girls showed up, JoJo foretold it."

Tracey made an indistinct noise in the back of his throat. I poured him a cup of coffee, adding some of the special honey because what the hell, he had done more than one favor for me over the past twenty-four hours.

"So, all's I'm saying is, why not use the resources you got?" Christine continued, oblivious to Tracey's inattention.

"We follow up on every lead," Tracey assured Christine. "And JoJo Sands has never called us." He scratched his chin with the tine of a fork and gestured at Daisy. "Her kid brother did, though. Goth Pigpen. He was the one who suggested we check out the woods, said we missed one."

I froze mid-way through pulling a plate of pancakes out of the kitchen window. "Wait—Matty Sands called in the tip about the girl? The girl you found a couple of days ago?"

"Dude!" Joanne insisted, rattling the pancake plate impatiently.

Tracey sipped his coffee calmly. "Yeah, told us he just had a feeling that there was another one out there and that we had to go get her."

Matty Sands, whom Daisy wouldn't wait on. Matty Sands, who showed up drunk and surly the night after the girl was found. Matty Sands who was inexplicably championed by none other than Corey Wilde. His sister may have been a crap psychic but Matty seemed to know some things he had no business knowing.

"Hey," Tracey said sternly, "you don't look like a woman thinking hard about onion rings."

I gave him my most waitress-y smile. "Tracey, I am never not thinking about onion rings."

· · ·

JoJo Sands lived and worked in a little yellow house on about an acre of unkempt land near the high school. Above the back door there was a hanging wooden plank with an upright palm carefully but amateurishly painted on it.

I didn't have an appointment, but I didn't think that mattered (she'd see me coming, right?) and when I pushed on the door, it swung open under my hand. Apparently psychics liked it real dark, because, when I walked inside, I could hardly see my own upturned hand in front of my face. My first impression was of an overwhelming smell of cat and an uncomfortable heat.

"Sorry," came a voice from the darkness, "heater's broke."

As my eyes adjusted, I began to make out the contours of the little room. An indistinct figure—I took it to be JoJo herself—was bent over a table, fiddling with something. I heard the metallic grind of a Bic lighter and a small flame appeared, floating in a little jarred candle.

"You want a reading?" she eyed me skeptically,

like she could tell that I wasn't exactly her usual client.

"Uh . . . kinda," I said. "My friend Christine—"

JoJo cut me off. "You're looking for a windfall? Lucky numbers? I can do a whole numerology chart for you. I'm running a special right now, twenty-five dollars. It's usually thirty-five, so that's a pretty good deal."

I started to answer, but my words were immediately drowned out by a spray of televised gunfire. "Shithead," JoJo muttered to herself. She glanced up at me, "Not you."

"I didn't figure."

"Hold on a sec," she said, moving across the room to a door I hadn't noticed before.

Light exploded into the room and I was rendered temporarily blind.

"Matty, if you don't turn that TV down I'm gonna beat your ass!" I heard JoJo shouting from the next room. A masculine voice answered her, just a sullen rumble.

I moved over to the door and opened it further. I could also see directly into the living room where all the furniture was covered in an informal sheath of discarded laundry. By far the newest and cleanest thing in the room was a large wall-mounted television. Matty had planted himself in front of it and I could see the back of his head, a halo of unwashed curls.

Without the door blocking me, I could hear him clearly. "It's my TV," he said, not looking toward JoJo who had adopted a beleaguered stance next to the arm of the sofa.

"Well it's my house and I'm trying to pay the fucking rent right now, so turn it down for forty minutes, okay?"

Matty raised a middle finger in response.

JoJo's hands moved swiftly but awkwardly, smashing the side of her fists against his ear, his shoulder, his skull in a flurry of blows. I was reminded of living with my mother and just about any of her boyfriends and the way that violence erupted from the ordinary in such a rapid, almost mundane fashion, until you started to think that was just the shape of the world.

Matty didn't seem too wounded by JoJo's assault however. "Ow!" he whined, leaning out of her reach, "cunt!"

"Turn down the TV!" JoJo shouted again.

If I wanted to watch people have bitter, violent fights I had my own estranged family members for that. "Hey, I think I'm going to have to get going—"

JoJo charged across the living room towards me. "No, no, we haven't even started yet!"

"I really don't want—"

The sound of gravel spraying interrupted me. JoJo and the kid on the sofa both stiffened up as though they'd heard the click of someone pulling a hammer back. Outside, a heavy car or truck door slammed and we all waited in silence as a pair of boots scuffed their way up the cement steps to the front door.

The man who opened the front door didn't look like the type to inspire watchful silence. He was slight and wiry, a full inch or two shorter than JoJo herself and he had a dopey little mustache that he probably imagined made him look more mature. He looked vaguely familiar, like he'd come in the diner once or twice.

"Get your damn bike out of the driveway, I almost ran it over," he spit at Matty, who still hadn't moved or turned. When the man made his way into the kitchen and spotted me standing there, his whole demeanor shifted. He offered me a welcoming smile.

"You here for Jo's palm-reading?" he asked. "You know, my girl here has a gift like most people can't imagine."

Behind us all, Matty cranked the volume on the TV as high as it would go.

"Actually," I said, straining to shout over the television, "I was hoping to talk to Matty."

Matty turned around and looked at me. His face

was just as sallow and irritable as it had been on the night of the diner fight and there was no recognition in it. "About what?" he shouted over the still-deafening TV. The mustache man and JoJo looked quizzically at one another.

"Turn that down, come outside, and I'll tell you."

Matty tossed his head like a fretful show pony but obeyed me, turning off the television with one click. He slouched to his feet and gestured exaggeratedly at the door.

Outside, Matty immediately dug a battered pack of Newports out of his pocket and lit one. It was an odd choice of cigarette for a young man and I figured he probably lifted them from his sister. "Okay, what?" he prompted. Charming.

"I don't know if you remember—"

"I remember. You're the waitress. From the diner," he added when I gave him a look. "Phoebe or whatever."

"Frannie, but that's not important. I just wanted to ask you about Ray and Corey."

He looked at me blankly.

"The meth-heads?" I prompted and that elicited a tiny smile.

"Yeah, I remember them too."

It would have been tough to forget.

"So you don't, like, know them personally or anything?" I probed, watching his face, which showed nothing in the way of emotion.

"Not really. Think I mighta seen the girl around or whatever but I don't know her. And, honestly, I don't know why she got up in the other chick's grill but I'm thankful." The smallest hint of vehemence crept into his tone. "That bitch was crazy."

"So you didn't grab her ass?" I asked him, remembering the laser-focused way he'd been staring at her that night.

"Why would I grab a stranger's ass?" Matty shot back. He did not, I noted, answer the question.

"Who would?" I agreed without agreeing.

"Really, I was just wondering if maybe they—or maybe someone else—had said something to you. What, with you being the one who called in that body out in the forest and everything."

Finally, an expression bloomed across Matty Sands's face: fear. "How did you get that information? Those tip lines are anonymous, they're not allowed to tell anyone. It's illegal for you to know that!"

"Hey, I'm just looking out for you here, kiddo. You know, because Ray Keene is actually kind of a psychopath and Corey isn't much better and if they thought that maybe someone had been ratting out some sort of, I dunno, *crime*, they probably wouldn't be too happy and—"

"Stop! Stop! Stop!" Matty raised up both of his hands up towards my face, like he was going to clamp them over my mouth but I gave him a warning glare and he leaned back. "It's not what you think. It's not anything like what you think."

He breathed out slowly, his whole body

shuddering with the effort of it. When he looked back up at me, I could swear there were tears in his eyes. "I had to call. She *made* me do it."

• • •

"So, Matty Sands is saying that a forest ghost—" Tracey's voice emanated disconcertingly from my crotch as I tried to drive and talk to him on speaker-phone at the same time.

"—he didn't say 'forest ghost,'" I interrupted. "Just that it was in the forest. And he didn't think it was alive."

"So a *forest ghost.* Which told him the location of a corpse?"

"That was the gist of it, yes."

"Okay, when I tell you that's not the stupidest thing I've heard all week, please don't allow that statement to in any way diminish how incredibly stupid that is. I just have a job that requires me to listen to a lot of stupid shit."

I smiled, in spite of myself.

"I know, I know. Obviously, he's lying but he did know where the body was, right?" I turned into the long driveway and started bumping my way towards home. "I don't actually believe that there's a ghost out in the woods."

"Well," Tracey laughed, "it wouldn't be the first time someone said—"

"Hold on." I didn't bother to turn the phone off as I stepped out of the car warily.

There was a light on in the kitchen, an almost homey yellow glow. I knew for a fact that I had not left the light on—Gramma hated nothing so much as wasting electricity.

"Frannie?" Tracey's voice was tinny and distant.

"Someone's been in my house." I listened for a moment, but couldn't hear anything but the distant sounds of frogs calling to one another in the gloaming.

I climbed the porch steps cautiously, still listening, still hearing nothing but ordinary country noise. Tracey must have heard the dull creaking of the wooden steps under my feet. "Frannie, hold on, don't go inside. I'm coming over," he insisted, practically yelling. I didn't bother to shut the phone off before sticking it in my back pocket and reaching for the door.

Forest Interlude

4

My girl, My girl, don't lie to me

Tell me where did you sleep last night?

In the pines, in the pines

Where the sun don't ever shine

I would shiver the whole night through

  —*In the Pines, traditional*

The only other person who ever saw me was also a little boy. He was a little older than the other one and his face was dirty. He was carrying a plastic shopping bag, clenched in his fist like he was worried someone was gonna take it off him.

At first, I thought he was like all the others but I followed him anyway. Maybe I did it because of the other little boy, who was never far from my mind.

My need to be recognized had only increased since him. It was like how sometimes a sip of water only reminds you how strong your thirst is.

When he came into the forest, he walked with purpose. The bag made a regular swishing crinkle as it swung back and forth next to him. He didn't look at me the way the other one had, but he stopped then and pricked up his ears. I didn't make any sounds, though, I know that for sure. There are many things that I cannot do in the forest but, out here in these trees, I can be very, very quiet.

He kept walking and I kept following until he reached a big pine that had been dropping its needles down in a skirt around its base. It was probably late, I realized, though I myself did not feel the passing of minutes or hours. But little kids were supposed to have bedtimes.

He sat under that tree with his knees pulled up and his plastic bag cradled protectively against his stomach. After a while, he started to sleep. Sitting there up against the tree bark with his vacant, unconscious face I thought he looked a lot like my body, still sitting vigil under another tree in this very forest. The things that made him different were so small: little, fragile rises and falls of his body, the heat that rose off of him like a glow. You had to get up real close before you could see where the blood was still moving inside him and coloring him slightly, instead of pooling at his lowest places like mine had. And of course he would, if he chose, be allowed to walk out of these trees and never come back again.

When he woke up, it was dark in the forest. He had brought a small flashlight like the kind that comes on a keychain. He rifled in his bag and came out with a candy bar that he ate like a wild thing, adding more smears to the finger painting on his chin and neck. When he was done, he looked around him and, for the first time, he seemed afraid.

I didn't try to touch him because what did I know about comforting after all? And the forest was a scary place, it was probably right for him to fear it.

I sat down beside him. I could see how tightly his small hands were clutching at the fabric of his jeans and I could see that each one of his fingernails was a thin crescent of dirt. It was something about those fingernails that called up one of my rare and incomplete memories.

I was very young, about the same age as the boy and I had run away from home. It wasn't a real running away, all I did was go to an abandoned house on the end of our dirt road. I remembered rolling out a Barbie sleeping bag on the floor and eating the Little Debbie snacks I brought as my provisions. I had also brought a can of tuna fish but forgot the can opener.

I don't remember why I ran away. I knew that I was angry, though. I could feel it, inarticulate and stifled. I had a fantasy about what my absence would mean. I imagined making them all—especially my mother—so afraid. I imagined coming back and just being . . . cherished. I imagined that I could somehow make myself precious by making myself scarce.

I stayed in that abandoned house for a long time, getting hungrier and more bored. I realized then that my mother wasn't going to call out the National Guard—wasn't even going to call the police. I realized that, instead of making her sorry, my absence was only making my mother's life easier.

I went home because I had no more food and because I knew then that, despite all my daydreams, I didn't have anywhere else to go.

When I went back, the house was empty. I don't remember what time of day it was or what I did after letting myself in but I remember clearly when my mother came in the door to find me on the sofa eating Ramen noodles I had made for myself.

She had not been looking for me. She had been doing whatever she did when she left me alone. I remember because she had the same smell, something it would take me a long time to identify as liquor. "Do that again," she told me, "and I'll beat your ass." And then she vanished into her bedroom.

I leaned toward the boy, who had buried his head

in his knees. "Go home," I whispered into his ear. "No one is looking for you."

He listened to me and I was sad as I watched the small figure of him, walking away through the trees, following the river back to the places he knew. I thought that might be the last I ever saw of him— and the last he ever saw of me.

It wasn't, though.

The first thing I noticed when I walked into the house was how mostly-intact everything was. My shoes were still lined up by the door, and the television set, which was so ancient it had bunny ears, was still tucked in the entertainment center. Even my water glass from the night before was sitting placidly on the coffee table.

The second thing I noticed was that Peter and Aleph's cage was open.

I moved through the rest of the house delicately, making the soft skittering noises I made when it was time to feed the two of them. I listened close for the sound of tiny movements but there was nothing. Then, I stepped into the kitchen where the overhead light was gleaming, and I saw it, right in the middle of the floor where I would be sure to find it—him.

I couldn't say which one of the rats it was. Peter was smaller and had a white spot on one leg but there was no making that distinction now. Whoever it was, he was just a smear of gray with a long, naked tail protruding from it. There was a light half-print in red leading across the kitchen towards the back door. The tread looked like something off a man's work boot.

I must have stayed crouched there for a while because the next thing I knew, Tracey was letting the screen door bang behind him as he ran through the house.

"Are you crazy, Frannie? You know I fished a dead body out of the woods not a quarter of a mile away from here, right? You could have been killed!" He stopped short when he found me in the kitchen.

I'd had Peter and Aleph for three years now.

They were a present from Devon for my sixteenth birthday. The only good present he ever got me. "Hand me the roll of paper towels by the sink," I said, my voice without inflection. "I gotta clean this up."

Tracey did as I asked and then got down on his knees to help me, glancing at the remains on the floor. "Was that your . . . ?"

I nodded.

"Shit, Frannie, I'm sorry."

"It's Ray Keene," I said, wrapping up what remained of a little creature who depended on me. I rolled the towel around him—a cheap, off-brand shroud.

"Frannie, you can't know that." I could tell that Tracey was trying hard to keep his voice gentle. I stood up and held the paper-wrapped bundle over the trash can but I just couldn't bring myself to toss him away.

Instead, I took down an old plastic container

that once held sandwich meat and put the bundle inside as delicately as I could.

"I can and I do," I said, turning to Tracey, who was still crouched on the floor, looking at the boot print. "He's fucking with me, trying to get in my head."

"Or it could have just been an ordinary thief. This house out in the middle of nowhere, it'd be an attractive target for some tweaker looking for cash."

"What burgling meth-head leaves all the valuable shit? Doesn't even bother to *look* for valuable shit, in fact?" I closed the plastic lid on Peter or Aleph. "And why would this random thief kill my rats?"

"Because they didn't like rats? I don't know, Frannie but you've got no reason to think that Keene had anything to do with this."

I shook my head. I could feel blood rising up in my cheeks and my neck. I always turned tomato-red when I got truly angry. "I do, though. I do. This is payback. I went into his house and took something of his so he broke in here and took something of mine."

"You took . . . " Tracey's eyes narrowed. "You took something from Ray's apartment?"

"It didn't really belong to him anyway. It was Shayna's drawing. I watched her do it."

Tracey ground the heel of his hand against his forehead. "I swear to god, Frannie, you are trying to get yourself killed," he muttered. "Look, why don't you grab your stuff and you can stay at my place tonight."

"What? No way. I'm staying right here."

"You can't stay here!"

"I can and I will. Ray Keene is not going to make me afraid in my own home. If it comes to it, I have the .22—"

"No! That's . . . that's actually insane, Frannie." He put a hand on my shoulder, which I immediately shrugged off. "I get it, you're proud and you're standing your ground or whatever but you can't—"

"You *don't* get it!" I roared, shocking him into

silence. "This is *my* place. Gramma, my mother, Devon and me, we all grew up in this house. I passed up *college* to stay here and pay the property tax because Gramma could not stand it—I couldn't stand it—this house leaving the family. *I* belong here. Ray Keene is the one who has no claim on this place and I'll be god-damned if I let him run me out of my own fucking home!"

While I was talking, I had somehow balled one hand into a fist and, as I spoke, I brought it down so hard on the edge of the kitchen table that the whole thing jumped and I felt a dull ache along the side of my pinky.

For a silent, heavy moment, Tracey just looked at me. "Fine," he said eventually. "Does that sofa in the front room pull out?"

. . .

"You really don't have to stay," I said, over slices of the delivery pizza that served as our dinner. "I don't need a babysitter." My eyes flicked to the service revolver bundled on his belt. "Or a gunslinger."

"I'm just protecting and serving, Frannie."

I snorted. "Well, I guess there's a first time for everything. But I would have to imagine that there are people a little bit more in need of protection right now, wouldn't you think?"

Tracey chewed contemplatively before answering in an uncharacteristically grave tone. "I know you're tough, Frannie, and you've been taking care of yourself for a long time, but a little bit of fear might do you some good when it comes to Ray Keene."

It was quiet. I pushed my uneaten pizza around on my plate.

"He killed those girls, didn't he?" I said finally. It was the truth that I had known in my belly from the moment I saw him, just standing next to Shayna and yet looking so *wrong*. Profane, almost.

"I don't know," Tracey admitted. "Ray's definitely a piece of shit but I'm not sure you can make the leap from piece of shit to serial murderer."

"Why not? It all fits. Ray moves around, going from state to state, truck stop town to truck stop town. He has plenty of access to women looking to get paid or looking for a ride. Women who are vulnerable. Who are willing to get in a truck alone with him." *Women like Shayna.* "And, whatever else happens, he always comes back to Our Lady. There's something that brings him back here and I don't think it's Corey Wilde. And what about that thing a few years ago? What was that girl, fourteen? Thirteen?"

"That family never pressed charges."

"Yeah," I drawled, "funny how that always seems to happen. What's the deal with the Sheriff's office and Ray Keene anyway? It's like he's invisible to you people. Does he got pictures of someone fucking a goat or what?"

Tracey shifted uncomfortably. "Don't try to bullshit me, Tracey," I warned. "We both know you can't."

Tracey heaved a sigh. "Okay, but don't tell

anyone I told you this. This isn't supposed to leave the department, you understand?"

I nodded.

"A few years ago, way before I joined the Sheriff's department, Sheriff Ogden got a hair up his ass about Ray Keene. He had it on good authority that Keene was helping various groups move crank and also that the recent 'theft' of Ray's rig had been one part package transfer and one part insurance scam.

"Ray was living in Corey's mother's trailer then and he kept an arsenal there. Wasn't afraid to use it, either. The boys knew that they had to come at him hard and in great numbers if they were going to take him in. They got extra dudes from other counties, dogs, SWAT gear, all the shit. What they didn't bother to do, I guess, was plug any leaks in the department.

"They found his place empty and about as clean as it got and when they were done searching, they came out to find that someone had lit one of their squad cars on fire.

"That wasn't the last 'mysterious' fire either. Two of the guys who went on the raid—guys who weren't even local deputies, mind you—had their houses catch fire. One guy wasn't home, the other one only barely got his wife and kids out. Then, a couple of months after that, two of the deputies just happened to get jumped outside The Taproom. One of them had a ruptured spleen, poor kid almost died."

"But isn't all that just more reason to lock his ass up?" I wondered.

"Well, they couldn't actually prove Ray was involved in any of it. Witnesses wouldn't talk, victims sure as hell wouldn't talk and Ray has friends, either whoever he was running drugs with or his crazy-ass hillbilly cousins or whatever. There wasn't any legal way to touch him and the illegal ways . . . well, he was better at that shit. Any LEO who set foot on his property could expect to be used for target practice."

"Couldn't you get some backup or whatever? Go to the state police?"

"Trust me, the sheriff tried. That deputy with the busted spleen? That was his second-oldest son. The state police don't give a shit what happens out here, Frannie. Money is draining out of this town and people are too. We got six deputies and I'm the only one under forty. In five years, three of them will have retired and there's no one to take their place. Every year, we get less money, fewer resources." Tracey shrugged. "Sheriff Ogden . . . he's just trying to protect the people he has left."

"Meanwhile, the bodies pile up out in the forest," I said flatly.

"We never found any evidence that would link Ray—"

"And how hard did you look, Tracey?"

He had the good grace to look at least a little ashamed. "We have a standing department-wide order not to . . . engage with Keene."

That explained why Tracey had gone so easy on

him that night in the diner. And why no one had helped Corey when she tried to get him on domestic violence charges. "So that's it? We just let him do whatever he wants whenever he wants?"

Tracey shook his head sadly. "The department does what it can to . . . mitigate the damage. I saw Sheriff Ogden give money from his own 401K to the family of that thirteen-year-old girl."

Tracey must have seen something in my face, horror, most likely. "What do you want, Frannie? You want me and the rest of the deputies to risk getting beat to death by meth-heads or having our house set on fire with us in it for the glorious promise of seventeen dollars an hour?"

I felt a pang at the idea. I imagined for a moment a bunch of biker-types jumping Tracey—I almost couldn't even picture him in a fight.

"No," I said softly, "that's not what I want." Even as I said it, though, I could not help but think again of Shayna and how her absence gnawed at me.

I thought of the lights in the forest and all the dead women who still had no names.

. . .

Tracey refused to sleep in Devon's old room—or even my room—if I was going to sleep on the couch downstairs. "I can't spend the night a floor above you, it defeats the purpose."

I raised my eyebrows at him.

"The purpose of *protecting* you. Someone could come in that door and fill you full of bullets before I even got down the stairs."

"Well, I can tell you right now that kind of talk definitely makes me feel safer," I said, digging around in Gramma's linen closet for the old sleeping bag I was pretty sure Devon had left here. "You're gonna have to pull up a piece of floor."

Tracey reached into the closet above me, bumping his chest up against my shoulder blades in a way that seemed unnecessarily familiar. He pulled a bulky green bundle down from the top.

"Won't be the first time I slept on this floor," Tracey said cheerfully and I could feel his breath on my neck and the side of my face.

I was uncomfortably aware of the fact that Tracey Finnerman would have sex with me, if given the opportunity. In fact, I had a sense that he regarded it as an inevitability. Maybe not tonight, but *some* night because what the hell else were the two of us going to do to pass the time in this little hick town?

When I was eleven or twelve, I thought I would marry Tracey someday. Partially, it was because he was the only boy I knew really well but mostly because he was good to me and life with my mother had taught me how rare sweetness was between a man and a woman. It was years before I figured out what that sweetness meant, the night I stitched up his head, in fact.

He had wrapped his arms around my waist and pressed his face into my belly (smearing blood all over my pajama top). "You take such good care of me, Frannie," he murmured and I knew then exactly what I was to him: someone to patch him up or sober him up, to make his excuses and clean up his messes. A soft place to land.

I stuffed the sleeping bag into Tracey's arm and pointed him towards a spot of floor beside the coffee table.

I flicked off the overhead light until just the lamp next to the couch was on, bathing the whole room in a sort of egg-yolk yellow light. Tracey waited for me to settle on to my couch-bed before hitting his own blankets. I turned off the last lamp and plunged the two of us into darkness.

Tracey was quiet for a long time, so long that I thought he was asleep. Then he said softly, "Frannie, Sheriff Ogden isn't a bad man. I want you to know that."

I wondered if he did want that, or if he wanted me to know that he wasn't following a bad man's orders.

"I'll talk to him, bring in some of the stuff you've found. Maybe there's something we can do. Get a warrant to search his truck, or talk to that Sands kid some more."

Oh yeah, Matty Sands. I rolled over until I was facing Tracey's direction. His face was probably about even with mine, just six or seven inches south. "What was it you were saying earlier about ghosts out in the forest?"

"You really never heard that? I think they told us the story every year at Boy Scout camp."

"You were a Boy Scout?" I couldn't help but laugh; the mental image of Tracey in one of those beige uniforms with the dorky kerchiefs was too wonderful.

"Well, I *was*. Until I met you and Devon. You guys were terrible influences."

"Us?" I gasped. "Tracey Finnerman, you were the one who gave me my first drink of liquor and my first joint and my first . . . lots of stuff."

I could hear him laughing, quiet and liquid. It

was easier somehow to talk to him like this, the two of us in the dark, not seeing one another but knowing we were close. So close that we could reach out and touch skin to skin, should either of us choose to do so.

"This ghost story is as old as the town itself. In fact, many people say that it was the ghost that gave this town its unusual name."

"I always thought it was a Catholic thing? You know, like Our Lady of Guadalupe?"

"Sorta. This happened back in pioneer days. When this was just a stop-over place for people who were headed west to California or Oregon."

"Gosh," I deadpanned. "How things have changed."

"This family, the Burns, came through on a wagon train. They were Irish Catholics with a shit-load of kids but the only one that really mattered was the youngest, a little boy. Like toddler aged."

"So, the whole wagon train was sort of . . . camping. I guess. And, somehow, the Burnses lost track of their youngest. He went out to play or look for cow patties to burn or whatever pioneer kids did and he just . . . never came back.

"They figured out pretty quickly that he was probably in the forest. Even now, today, it would be almost impossible to find a little kid out there. And this was before all the logging in the 1900s, so the forest was probably two or three times the size it is now.

"But Ma and Pa Burns weren't accepting that. They were prepared to park their wagon and wait until their son came back to them.

"The rest of the wagon train couldn't wait with them, though. They had to get across the mountains before the weather turned or they'd be stuck until the next year. So they gave the Burns family what supplies they could spare, said their goodbyes and moved on.

"They were there for months, through the bad weather and out the other side and, as the story goes, they still went out every day, splitting into groups and canvassing the forest.

"And then one day, almost exactly a year later, the littlest Burns came walking out of the forest wearing the same clothes he wore when he vanished and looking, in fact, exactly the same as he had a year before.

"Obviously the Burnses were overjoyed and by all accounts the boy was completely normal and unharmed, except that his clothes were all soaking wet. They asked the boy over and over again to explain what happened to him, where he'd been so long, how he'd survived, why he didn't seem to have aged at all and he only ever had one answer for them: he was with the lady from the river.

"The way the boy told it, he had gone into the forest to play and fell into the river. He was saved by a young woman who never said a word to him. She picked him up out of the water and then, the boy said, she laid down in the dirt beside him and the two of them took a nap. As soon as he woke up, he walked back out of the woods. He insisted that he was only gone a couple of hours, an afternoon at most.

"It wasn't exactly a satisfying story, as you'd imagine, so the Burns thought up another explanation, one that made sense to them: their son had been saved by a miracle, a special intervention from the Virgin Mary herself. And thus the name of the town."

"At the Boy Scout camp—which, by the way, was in the state forest—they always ended the story by telling us to be careful in the woods because sometimes the lady got lonely and took a wayward boy. Trapped him somehow," Tracey added in a spooky rumble.

I laughed but, all of a sudden, I could not help but remember the real anguish in Matty Sands's voice. *She made me do it.*

Forest Interlude
5

In my dreams she still doth haunt me,

Robed in garments, soaked in brine;

Then she rises from the water

And I kiss my Clementine.

—*My Darling Clementine, traditional*

The boy's mother killed herself, though I might have been the only person who knew that. She picked a narrow, sparsely travelled dirt road that wound through the trees for part of its length. Then she found a huge old tree that has probably been growing since before this place had a name and pointed her little two-doored car right at it and hit the gas.

I knew it was the boy's mother because I had seen

her plenty of times before. Ever since that first night when he came into the woods with everything he thought he'd ever need, things had passed between us. Mostly feelings. He was angry, he was afraid, he was happy, he was sick, he was angry, he was afraid. But sometimes I saw whole moments, the strongest ones where the emotions were concentrated into something thick and bitter.

I saw his mother crying during the daytime as she laid on a bare mattress, just a sheet resting over her shivering body. When he went to her and asked if she was going to get up, she reached for him and pulled him into the bed, half a hug, half a strangle. She wasn't wearing any clothes and the boy could feel how hot, how feverish the skin underneath her breast was. Every part of her was sweating. The boy fell asleep there and, when he woke up, he found that she had vomited in the bed and it was touching the ends of his hair.

Just before she hit the tree, long after she could

have braked, she looked through the windshield at me. And she saw me.

I think I was the last thing she saw.

· · ·

The bleed-through went both ways and the boy didn't like it. It hurt him and made him feel ashamed. The pieces of my life that I could recall were nightmares to him or inexplicable things that emerged just to torment him. I thought about the cold of the river and he shivered. I remembered the feeling of something thin and immovable and cutting around my throat and he scrambled for his inhaler. I recalled the misery of my first periods and he cramped and sweat on his bathroom floor.

He hated it—I always knew when he hated things—but I didn't care because even if he never set foot in the forest again, I knew that he knew about me. He saw me even when he didn't want to look. He heard me even when he tried not to listen.

I didn't know how to take the sting out of my memories. Sometimes it seemed the ones that hurt the most were always the strongest. So I tried, instead, to offer him some things in exchange.

I showed him all the best things in the forest, the places where people left things, either because they had been careless or because they didn't want them found. Half-empty bottles of the good whiskey, baggies of pot wrapped tenderly in tin foil like little Christmas presents, rolls of fives and tens crammed into coffee cans, anything I thought someone might want.

I showed him other things too, secrets people kept. I showed him the little clearing where his geometry teacher took the fifteen-year-old girl he was diddling and the pond where a girl named Irene allowed her friend Sharon to drown. Sharon called out to her, but Irene stood dripping on the shore and pressing her knees together like she was trying to banish an urge to pee. He was confused when I showed him that, he couldn't recognize the girls as I saw them, the sun on their slick, dark hair and not yet women. I think they were older when he knew them. I think he figured it out eventually, though. He wasn't stupid, the boy, though he was very stubborn.

Secrets are a kind of currency of their own and I don't know if what I offered to him was equal in value to the things I pushed on him but I always did my best and I can't say the same for him. He didn't seem to care that I knew about seemingly every twitch of his tweenage libido. He didn't seem to mind that I saw the vicious dreams he had about the girls in his class, dreams where he sat on their chest, like an old hag that steals your breath, and pulled out their long, dark hair in chunks. He never seemed bothered that I saw the times when those dreams were about his mother or his older sister, and that those moments were the most vivid, the most indelible.

I suppose that it was only fair, then. He would not have chosen me but I would not have chosen him and no one would have chosen to remain in this forest, alone and unseen, slowly ceasing to exist.

6

I woke up the next morning with pancakes on my mind.

Tracey was still sleeping. He pressed his face so hard into one pillow and clutched another one to him—he was like a big, fierce child. It was good of him, I thought, to stay here on my floor and look out for me, as useless as that was.

Despite what Tracey might have thought, I wasn't delusional. I knew what would happen if Ray Keene decided he really and truly wanted to hurt me and it would happen whether or not Tracey was sleeping on my floor. Still, the gesture was a kind one and it seemed to deserve some manner of reward.

I got up as quietly as I could and started scrounging in the kitchen for pancake fixings. It was there, behind the old flour canister that I found my first real flicker of joy since I'd noticed Shayna was gone from the diner. It was Aleph, curled up behind the flour canister, almost like he was hiding but probably because that cupboard was over the stove light and was always warm.

He squeaked happily when he saw me and I extended my hand out to him, allowing him to run along it and up to my shoulder. It was the sort of moment where a person might cry, if they were the crying sort of person.

"Hey little fella," I said, touching his long, skinny tail. "You got away from him, didn't you? Smart one." His small body was warm and soft on the skin of my neck and I swear it felt almost like he was nuzzling me. I let him perch there and hummed tunelessly while I gathered up the rest of the ingredients.

I was so preoccupied that I didn't even notice when Tracey woke up.

"You cooking with a rat on your shoulder?" he asked sleepily. "You know that shit's only cute when Cinderella does it."

"Found him in the cupboard," I said, not even bothering to hide my grin.

My cell phone, plugged into the wall charger, began to jingle. I pressed it between my ear and shoulder, still working on the pancakes. "Hello?"

"Hey Frannie? It's Daisy. From work."

"Hey Daisy . . . what's up?" For a second, I wondered if I could have somehow mixed up my days in all the recent confusion and left her alone with a big weekend crowd.

"Hey, um, did you like . . . go and interrogate Matty Sands?"

"I wouldn't say interrogate—"

"Because he called me. He's really pissed and he

thinks I told you stuff about him, which I tried to tell him I didn't, but he was really convinced, and I just wanted to tell you that you should probably leave him alone."

I stepped away from the pancake batter and positioned the phone more effectively. "Daisy, did he threaten you?"

"No! I just . . . I don't want to have anything to do with this. With him."

"You aren't, though. I didn't mention your name to him."

"Yeah, but he's always going to think that I had something to do with it because I know about—" she cut herself off. "Stuff," she said instead in a small voice. "Just . . . don't go over there again, okay? Matty's not . . . the helpful type."

"JoJo Sands's house is the first place I'm headed this morning if you don't explain what the hell you're talking about."

Tracey quirked an eyebrow at me and dipped his

thumb into the pancake batter. "Gross," I mouthed silently at him. He licked his thumb and shrugged.

On the other end of the phone, Daisy sighed and lowered her voice so much she was practically whispering. "I just don't think it's a great idea to get Matty riled up."

"Why the hell not?"

"Because he . . . he has the way of . . . I don't know how to describe it." She sounded frustrated and I could picture the exact face she was making, the same one she made when I tried to teach her how to use the elderly and idiosyncratic cash register at the diner.

"Okay, so, I'm not proud of this but I wasn't a very nice kid growing up. There were these girls who everyone liked. They were the pretty ones, still are, actually. Kaitlyn Reed, Elle McCormick, Dini Mills . . . they were the cool people, the people to be with and the messed up part was, they liked me already. I didn't have to try very hard to be friends with them and I think it was because, at that age, it's easier to fool people into thinking you were . . . something you weren't.

"They all had money, those girls and I didn't. I never let them come over to my house and I used to walk home from school so they wouldn't see my mom's car when she came to pick me up."

"The most important thing, though, was distancing myself from the kids like Matty Sands. He was . . . well, Matty was poor. Not poor like me but poor like you'd imagine it. He had this ratty red hoody that he would wear literally for days. He didn't wash and he smelled. People used to make fun of him, say he had fleas, like a dog. He used to bring these weird packed lunches. Like, an entire two liter of Mountain Dew and a bunch of peanut butter crackers.

"I was a bitch to him," Daisy said flatly. "I admit it. I was mean for the sake of meanness and it all wound up not mattering anyway because my ninth birthday came and . . . well, that's a different story.

But the point was, I was bad to Matty and he was probably right to hate me.

"For a long time, though, I didn't know he hated me. He never fought back, he just sort of stewed and curled up inside himself. I guess he was just . . . waiting all those years, long after I'd fallen out with those girls and after everyone had more or less started ignoring him. Then he found me on the playground one day . . .

"He told me—" Daisy's voice caught a little bit in her throat "he told me that my Grandma Irene was going to die. And that she was going to hell. He told me that, when she was a little girl, about my age, she killed her friend, a girl named Sharon. He said they were swimming in the creek together and . . . and Grandma could have saved her but she was too scared to get back in the water. He said Grandma lied to everyone and said that she dived down under the water and when she came up, Sharon was gone. But that wasn't true, he said.

Grandma stood there on the shore and watched her die."

"It sounds like he was fucking with your head," I said.

Daisy's voice was reluctant. "Yeah . . . but my Grandma *did* die soon after that. She had a fall, broke her shoulder and never really recovered. We all took shifts, around her bed before she went and there was this one time when . . . when we were alone, just for an hour or so. But I had to ask her, Frannie. It was eating me up inside."

"What did she say?"

"She didn't say anything," Daisy said flatly. "She didn't have to. I saw the way her face changed when I said Sharon's name. It was true, Frannie, everything Matty Sands told me was true and how could he possibly know that, Frannie?"

She sounded pleading, as though she were just longing for me to give her an answer that made sense of the world again. "There are ways," I reassured her. "He could have heard some old gossip.

Or maybe your grandma and her friend weren't actually alone in the forest that day."

"Yeah," Daisy's voice flattened and sank. "That's what Matty said. He said *she* was there and that she was always watching."

●　●　●

JoJo was ready for us this time, sitting on the concrete slab that served as a front porch. Big night, I guessed from her giant sunglasses and the can of Miller Light she had pinned between her thighs.

When Tracey and I stepped out of the car, her eyebrows moved like she was narrowing her eyes at us. "We don't want any," she called out, only half-sarcastically.

"Hey JoJo," I said in my cheeriest waitress voice. "Matty in?"

"Sleeping."

The silence was awkward. "Can you get him up?"

"Why? What business do you have with my brother?"

"I need some help. I'm looking for a girl and I think he might know where she is."

"He doesn't." JoJo took a long, pointed sip from her beer can. "He doesn't have anything to do with any of that."

"Then why did he call in the tip about the woman in the forest?" I took few cautious steps towards the porch. JoJo didn't stop me but her body stiffened up the way a cat's will when it spots a strange dog.

"Look, you all found that girl and now you're done. There's no more. Let him be."

"There's more. There's one more, her name is Shayna. She's about your brother's age." I stepped up on to the porch proper and I knew exactly what kind of nasty look JoJo was giving me even through those dark glasses. Back on the lawn, Tracey was getting antsy.

"No," she shook her head. "There's all the ones

they found, the one from a couple of days ago and . . . "

"And then what?" I pressed.

"And then the other one. That junkie girl," she said, lowering her voice so Tracey could not hear.

"What the hell are you doing?" I turned to see Matty Sands standing in the open door wearing boxers and a too-small bathrobe with a Spiderman logo on it.

"Matty," I said, but he wasn't looking at me. He was looking at his sister with undisguised contempt and something that might have been a little bit of hurt as well. "What are you telling them, JoJo?"

"I'm telling them to leave you the fuck out of it," she snapped. "So go back inside."

"No," he roared. "You're throwing me under the bus, aren't you? You'd just love it if I got hauled off to jail. Fucking forget all about me and you can do whatever you want—"

"Why would you go to jail?" I demanded at the

same time that JoJo shouted, "I already do what I want!"

"You think I have to keep you here? Because I don't. I could send you to live with Dad in that fucking gator-infested swamp, you want that?" she seethed.

"You're gonna kick me out, really? For some scumbag?" he lowered his voice to a whisper when he said "scumbag" and glanced behind him.

"You don't know what you're talking about," JoJo stood up, abandoning her can of beer. "I'm trying to *help* you, you idiot." She poked him in the chest hard enough to make him rock back on his heels.

"Uh, Frannie . . . " Tracey began, climbing the steps to stand next to me. "Do you want me to—" he started in a low voice before stopping to look down at his belt in consternation. "Phone's vibrating," he said, retreating back down the steps. "I'll just be a second."

I figured it was a work thing, from the way he

strode across the lawn to a place where we couldn't hear him and turned away, back towards the road.

"No one is in trouble," I said in very calmest voice. "No one is going to jail. Please, just chill out. I only want to ask you a couple of questions, person to person. I'm not a cop or anything, I'm just a waitress."

Matty still looked doubtful but he didn't argue with me, so I continued, making my voice soft. "I don't think you've done anything wrong. I just think you might be able to help me find someone. From what I understand, you have a knack for . . . knowing things?"

He shook his head, not necessarily in disagreement but more like an animal might shake its head when trying to remove some constraint, like a bridle or a muzzle. "It doesn't work like that," he said. "She does whatever she wants and I just have to take it."

"It's not good for him," JoJo agreed. "He was sick for weeks before they found that girl. Couldn't keep food down, couldn't sleep. He was wasting away."

Matty scowled at her but didn't seem to particularly disagree.

"It . . . hurts you?"

He didn't meet my eyes but nodded.

"All the time." He sounded young when he said it, as young as Daisy. Which, of course, he was. "I feel like a . . . goddamn tweaker or something. Like there's something moving underneath my skin. Things . . . eating me every hour of the day. And that's when she's in a good mood."

Silently, JoJo reached down and retrieved the can of beer. She handed it to Matty who drank gratefully. "What happens when she's not in a good mood?" I asked but Matty said nothing, just kept drinking until the can was empty. He threw it down and it made a hollow crackle on the cement porch.

"And she showed you where the body was?"

"Not *showed* exactly. But she knew so I knew. Not that any of this is my problem," he added, his

153

voice taking on that familiar sulky teenage tone. "I don't know those girls."

No one knew those girls. The only names they had were the ones we gave to them. They were strangers but their killer had made them a part of this town—a part of us—when he abandoned them here.

"As far as I'm concerned," Matty stepped on the empty beer can, crushing it under his bare heel, "those girls were all fucking Darwin Award candidates anyway. Who gets into a car with some random stranger? And then they're surprised when he turns out to be a psycho?"

I half expected JoJo to chide him again, but she seemed to find nothing objectionable about this assessment. "Last I checked, we don't have the death penalty for hitchhiking," I said mildly.

"Hitchhiking," Matty snorted. "The girls were all probably truck stop hookers or junkies. Or both."

"Doesn't mean they deserved to go missing. To

go nameless. To lie out there in the forest until they turn into bones."

"Look, I don't know anything else. I haven't . . . gotten anything from her since they found that body and I'd like to keep it that way. My life is a whole lot better when she shuts up."

I was about to tell him that he might not have a choice, that none of us did, when Tracey appeared again at the base of the porch. His face was the color of chalk, making all of his freckles stand out in painful relief. I'd never seen him look that way before and I didn't like it at all.

I moved down the steps and touched his arm. "Tracey?"

He tilted his face towards mine but his eyes weren't looking at me, not really. "Corey Wilde is dead."

Forest Interlude

6

Poor Ellen Smith, how she was found

Shot through the heart lying cold on the ground

Her clothes were all scattered and thrown on the ground

And blood marks the spot where poor Ellen was found

—*Poor Ellen Smith, traditional*

I had never seen another dead thing in the forest before which, when I thought about it, was incredible. Things die all the time. Baby birds pushed from the nest too early, coyotes grown too old and scroungy to carry on, dogs and cats clipped on the freeway that crawled into the trees to die in a private place. Instead, it was like the forest was constantly being scrubbed clean, constantly presenting me with the most pristine version of itself. The only blemish on its surface was my own body, refusing to sink into the dirt.

So when I saw the other woman, I was confused. At first, I thought it was my own body, which still somehow managed to surprise me.

I remembered enough of myself to know that the other woman was older than I had been and her hair—when she had hair—was blonde and mine had been brown. I had been confronted so many times by then with my own remains. I'd had brown hair, dirty and tangled with leaves. Brown eyes, staring and cloudy.

I tried to ignore the other woman at first. And the forest let me. Or at least it let me get away from her body. Her presence, though, was like a mosquito trapped in a bedroom at night: a low, dull whine that becomes a fixation because it's surrounded by nothingness.

I looked for a version of the other woman that was like myself—not that I really knew what I looked like now. Would she be a shadow, moving strangely all by itself? A puff of smoke? A smell? A feeling? A strange disruption in the air the way gasoline will rainbow and gleam when it hits water? Whatever I might have been, I found no evidence that she was anything like me. I never found anything of her, in fact, except the shell she left behind.

And then I started to smell it. It had been so long since I had smelled anything that I couldn't help but relish it, even though it was terrible. Her decaying body smelled awful and it created a cascade of memories, all the noxious things I'd ever smelled before. Uncleaned outdoor toilets, a baby's diaper gone too long between changings, a huge man whose name I could not remember dead in a bathroom. Death had swollen him even more and he smelled not just like rot but also like sickly shit, like the kind of bowel movements a dying dog might have. All these things were so immediate they felt like burning. It almost felt like I was breathing again.

It was awful and it was constant but it felt so good to breathe again.

. . .

She was the first—but maybe only the first that I could remember. In any event, there were others. Some were younger, some were older. Some were bones. Some were so fresh and new that I had to kneel down beside them and try, as best I could, to touch them. They might have been sleeping.

But they weren't.

There were the sisters, who rested in each other's arms, like each was giving comfort to the other. I wondered if I would have liked that, having someone at the end. I wondered if it would have been worse, knowing that someone I loved was suffering with me. I wondered if I had any sisters. I wondered if they looked for me.

Sometimes people—living people—came to get them. Some of the people were very tender, they treated the women like they were mothers and sisters and lovers and friends and when they moved their bones. It was like an apology. Some of them were not gentle and moved the women like they were garbage or debris. After they were done, they would hold their hands out from themselves, as far as they could get from their own bodies.

It was funny to me now, how wide the gulf was for them between the living and the dead. Did they really think their body was made of anything different? Did they really believe that anything else would happen to them when they laid down in the dirt?

●　●　●

They never came for the first one, though. The one with the strongest smell. The one I kept finding over and over again, like the forest was leading me back to her. I was so . . . *aware* of her all the time. She did not belong, I decided eventually. The forest didn't want her the way it wanted me (wanted me so bad that it kept drawing me back and back and back no matter how many times I tried to get away).

She should have been taken away with the others. They hadn't seen her, though, they walked past her the way the hikers and old men fishing walked past me.

She was the first thing that hurt me since I'd come to the forest. I felt her like an old injury, like a bum knee or a bad back that puts you down when the air gets too cold or too damp. I felt it the most in my throat.

It was almost a sad thing, when they came in the darkness with their long black bags and their flashlight beams to collect her. I didn't like the pain but it was good to be reminded what flesh was, what hurt was.

What *I* was, before.

7

We sat in my car, doors shut for at least the illusion of privacy. Tracey was still looking out the windshield at nothing, but his face had a little more color now.

"They don't know for sure," he said, his voice creaky. "But Stuart said it looked like a heroin overdose."

"But you don't think so?"

Tracey swallowed hard, his eyes were glittering wetly. "I knew Corey since we were in diapers. Heroin . . . it wasn't her thing. That's what her mom used to get fucked up on back in the day.

Corey told me about how her mom would nod out and Corey would find her and think she was dead . . . she hated it."

"So . . . what do you think happened?" It didn't feel right, just saying what I imagined we were both thinking: *Ray Keene. Ray Keene fucking killed her the way we knew that he would.*

"I think I need to go into the Sheriff's office," Tracey said dully.

"Okay," I put my key in the ignition, "I'll drive you."

* * *

After I dropped Tracey at the Sheriff's office, I drove immediately back to JoJo's place. I was stuck on what she'd said to me about "the junkie" who was going to be added to the victim roster. Did she mean Corey and, if so, was there maybe a way to find out who Ray was going to target next?

When I pulled up, there was a suitcase and a

pile black plastic garbage bags out on the cement porch. There was no sign of JoJo but Matty was there, pounding on the door and yelling something I couldn't hear.

He bee-lined for the car as soon as he saw me, throwing open the passenger door and jumping inside like a bank robber making a messy getaway. "Go!" he said and I put the car in reverse. I was half-way down the driveway before I asked him where the hell we were going.

"Anywhere. Wherever you want." He pulled a small black flask from the pocket of his saggy jeans and drank desperately from it.

"JoJo kick you out?"

Matty picked his fingernails. They were bitten down practically to the quick and more than one of them was crusted with dried blood. A nervous kid. "She gets like this sometimes. Throws a shitfit and says I have to leave but she always calms down."

I turned right on Forest Avenue which led, as the name implied, to the state forest. Specifically to the part of the forest nearest my house, the part where they had found the most recent girl.

"Where are you going?" Matty asked, crinkling up his eyebrows.

"I thought you didn't care?"

"I don't want to go to the forest." He sat forward, still hunched but tensed up like he was preparing for an accident. "I don't go in there."

"Ever?" Going out to the remains of the big lumber mill from the 1930s and getting hammered had been a rite of passage when I was in high school.

"Once," Matty shook his head. "When I was little."

"Well, we're gonna go in today. We're going find your girl and we're gonna ask her how to stop Ray Keene."

I could feel Matty's incredulous look even without turning my head. "Ray Keene?"

"Ray Keene," I turned on to the old lumber road that led back into the heart of the trees, "is killing girls and leaving them in the forest. He took a friend of mine and I'm going to get her back."

Matty looked out the window, frowning at the trees overhead. There was a skittish energy to all of his movements, like a man making a very unsafe drug deal. "I don't know anything about that. Just the bodies."

"Well, maybe there's more that she can tell you."

"There isn't!" Matty pounded his fist on the dash. "I can't just ask her questions, I'm not your fucking psychic friend!"

I stopped the car at a slightly widened point in the road, a pullout of sorts and turned to look at him. "What you are is the best and only chance I have of finding Shayna before Ray Keene kills her. So you are going to help me or I'm going to have my friends at the Sheriff's office arrest you."

It was a total and complete bluff, but I recalled how quickly he had leapt to the specter of prison earlier.

"Arrest me for what?" he sneered.

"First degree being a douchebag? I don't know but I'm real creative. You're what, sixteen? Depending on the judge, that's close enough to try as an adult . . . "

His eyes widened and I knew I had him. "You are a crazy bitch," he said, half disbelief and half resignation.

I clipped the keys to my belt loop and opened the door. "Yeah, well, maybe you shouldn't get in cars with strangers."

* * *

"This is the spot where the body was, right?" I could still see the flattened brush from where the police vehicles had been and there was a ribbon of yellow caution tape caught in the lower branches of the tree.

"Never been," Matty said, slurring slightly. He'd partaken pretty liberally of his flask along the way.

"But you know what it looks like?"

Matty laughed. "It wasn't even her body, you know. I don't know where she died. I don't even know if she's really a person."

I thought about Tracey's story, about the Lady of the forest and how she was here, waiting, before the first white settlers crossed the Missouri River.

Whatever she was—if she even existed—she had so far given the only reliable information I had about the dead women and even if it was useless, even if it was all the warped imaginings of a teenage boy from a bad home, I had to try.

Matty half-sat and half-collapsed on the forest floor. He held one hand out to steady himself and used the other to clutch his flask. "Sit down," he muttered.

I did as he asked, sitting across from him in the dirt and watching his face for any sign of . . . well, anything. Knowledge from the other side, intent listening, visions. Whatever. Instead, he just looked kinda drunk and like his face was breaking out a bit.

"What are we doing?"

"I don't fucking know!" Matty said, way too loudly. "Waiting, I guess."

"Waiting for what?"

Matty took a long drag from his flask, more like a gulp than anything else. "You'll know," he grimaced.

* * *

We sat there like that for a long time. Matty emptied his flask and tucked it back into his pants. He hung his head over his limp hands and swayed gently.

Then, after what felt like an endless stretch of quiet, he reached out for me, fumbling at my hands. "What's going on?" I asked, allowing him to take both of my hands in his.

"I have to warn you," he mumbled, "that it's gonna hurt. It always hurts."

I didn't *hear* anything except for the sounds of the forest settling and the animals going about their business but, after a few moments, I began to feel something. I thought it might be that sensation he was talking about, that *eating* feeling. I tried to pull my hands away to itch . . . just everywhere, but Matty held on to them tight.

The feeling seemed to spread through me, starting at my hands and suffusing outwards like a drop of ink in a glass of water. I felt a numb buzziness and my teeth were . . . loose and strange. If I had reached up right then, I felt sure that I could have plucked one out with my fingers.

I felt too hot, though I knew that the forest was cool in the late afternoon. Sweat began to bead up on my chest, under my arms, on my upper lip. I could smell it and it didn't smell right, it didn't smell like me. It smelled . . . sickly. It smelled like a dead thing.

"Ask her about a girl named Shayna," I rasped.

Matty shook his head with dreamy slowness and muttered something. I tried my hardest to listen.

"Smell like . . . stale air and fuel. Laminate seats, the kind that stick to the back of your legs in the summer heat. He puts his hand between her thigh and the seat like he means to keep her from burning. But he doesn't."

I felt then a sudden stab of adrenaline, a fear that started in my chest and radiated outward in a steady, bloody pulse. It was the kind of fear I'd only felt a few times before, all in my childhood. *He slid his hand between the seat and her skin and he was touching her and she knew, she knew everything.*

This is what happened to her, I thought. To Shayna or to the woman they found out here or to the others without names.

"Tell me how to stop him."

Another feeling rose up within me, this one slightly dimmer, slightly duller. A sensation of loss, of hopelessness.

"Can't stop. She only tells the truth. If she says it, it happens."

I felt a different sense now of something looped around my throat. It pulled tighter and tighter and I wanted to reach up and grab it with my fingers but Matty was holding my hands, holding them so much tighter than I would have imagined he could. I writhed, anchored to him at the palms and my eyes were open but I could see nothing but black. My body arced up into the air like something was trying to rise out of me and fly away to safety.

And then, abruptly, I was entirely myself again. Matty had released my hands and he was watching me with an almost clinical interest. I was curled, I realized, in a fetal position in the dirt. I sat up slowly and rubbed my throat, disbelieving.

And Matty chuckled.

"What are you laughing about?" I cradled my hands in my lap, they ached from Matty's grip and I noticed that there were raging pink half-moon divots where nails had sunk into the skin on the back of my hand. *Matty*, I thought stupidly, *didn't have any fingernails.*

"I've just never seen it from the outside before. Hurts like a son of a bitch, huh?"

I realized then that he had done it on purpose.

He wanted to hurt me like he hurt. "Is that all we're gonna get?"

"I'd say so, yeah. She's not really a *friendly* ghost. Personally, I just think she doesn't want garbage and shit in her forest."

"Garbage," I repeated softly, thinking again of Shayna and how she used to draw portraits of the regulars and shyly offer them up.

"Not, like, *garbage*," Matty backpedalled insincerely. "But no one wants a dead body sitting around."

I got to my feet, jelly-knee'd. "If she's so set on having a clean forest, why not help us stop him?"

Matty shrugged, reached absently for the flask and then remembered that it was empty. "Maybe he's already done?"

. . .

"She was pregnant, you know." Matty had laid his face against the cold glass of the window. He was looking a little pale and I thought about pulling a few unnecessary stop-and-starts but I had no desire to hose vomit out of my car tonight. "The one I called in."

"Jesus Christ," I murmured, staring straight ahead.

"Isn't it almost . . . better this way?" Matty's voice was unsteady but earnest. "Better for the baby, I mean."

I turned my attention briefly from the road to give him the full effect of my incredulous look. "No, I don't think being murdered and dumped in the woods is better for anyone in any scenario."

"My mom died when I was a kid. Would have been better off if she did it before I was born." He gave me a sidelong look. "You never wished your mom didn't have you?"

I wished a lot of things about my mother.

" . . . no," I said.

"C'mon . . . " he wheedled, like he was trying to talk me into a rich dessert. "You don't think everyone's life would have been better if your mom didn't have some dealer's rape baby when she was seventeen?"

I went so still that the car glided almost to a halt before I remembered to keep pressing the gas pedal. "What the fuck are you talking about?"

"Your mom, your brother . . . you didn't know?"

I didn't and Matty knew that from the way he was grinning at me. It was the same smug grin he'd worn in the forest.

"Nope," I said as casually as I could manage. "My mother didn't talk much about that part of her life." I knew that she got pregnant with Devon in high school but I had always assumed her boyfriend at the time was the father. That was what Gramma seemed to believe as well. I wondered if it would have changed anything between the two of them, knowing . . . but that was pointless speculation. Gramma was dead and my mother was as good as dead. There were no amends to be made.

"*She* knew. She knows the truth about

everything. She was the one who told me that my mom killed herself. It was the only nice thing—the only *motherly* thing—she ever did for me."

"What about JoJo?"

Matty's face darkened. "What about her?"

"Hasn't she been a mother to you all these years?"

"Bullshit. She did everything she could to avoid taking me after mom died. I spent almost a year in foster care while she dicked around. All because her piece of shit boyfriend—which is different than the piece of shit boyfriend she has now—didn't want kids."

I thought about the way she had leapt to his defense when Tracey and I came to the door and the eggshells the two of them both walked on when her boyfriend was around and I figured that there was probably more to the story than Matty was letting on.

He was on a tear though, now. "If JoJo was smoking meth like that dead girl, everyone would tell her what a stupid, neglectful whore she was all the time. But because she likes guys who knock her around, because sometimes she shows up with a black eye and some crocodile tears, suddenly she's some great fucking hero.

"The ones in the forest are the same way. Just like my mom. Just like yours."

"I don't know." I found myself modulating my voice carefully. I had all the power in this car, my hands were on the wheel and my foot was on the pedal but it had nevertheless somehow started feeling . . . delicate, sort of. Perilous.

"And then those kids grow up and just do the same shit all over again. And people actually try to use that as an excuse, oh, you know, she had a bad childhood, you can't really blame her, blah, blah, blah. But I could have forgiven her if she'd grown up in a normal house. Then, at least she could say that she didn't know what she was in for."

I felt a strange sort of relief when we turned into JoJo's driveway. In the beam of the headlights, I could see that all those bags were still sitting out on the porch and the windows were dark. "Hey, are you sure you want me to drop you here?"

"Where else would I go?" He just sat there for a moment, and I debated how exactly to kick him out, but then he spoke in a voice that was soft and low and almost sort of . . . fond. Nostalgic, even. "You know she used to make me sleep in her bed when she still lived at home. She thought that me being there might keep Mom's fuckwad of the week out. Sometimes it worked.

"And we used to lay there in the dark and wait for him to go to sleep . . . it only got quiet in the house when he passed out . . . and she told me 'I'll never be with a man like that. I'd kill myself first.' That's what she said. I'd *kill myself* first."

Finally, he unlocked the door and pushed it open with his foot. Inside the house, someone must have noticed us and the porch light flickered on, dull yellow and already attracting bugs. Matty just stared at it. "But look at her," he said, genuine sadness in his voice. "She's still breathing, ain't she?"

. . .

Tracey's car was in the driveway when I finally trudged back home. I found him posted up on the front porch the way Gramma used to do when I was a teenager staying out late. "Where have you been?" he demanded, also much like Gramma.

"I've been where I've been, *Dad*." I climbed the steps while he peered disapprovingly at the mud caked on my pants.

"I'm serious, there is a serial killer running around and you're out . . . playing in the woods with Matty Sands."

"If you knew where I was, why bother asking?"

"I called JoJo when I couldn't find you." Tracey stood up angrily. "I should say I called JoJo after calling every other person who might know where you were because you went fucking AWOL and didn't answer your cell phone when *there is a serial killer on the loose!*"

"If you're so worried about it, how about you go do your fucking job and arrest Ray Keene?" I snapped.

Tracey looked down and I knew immediately that the Sheriff's office was not planning to look at Keene for these murders.

"Tracey, he just murdered his girlfriend!"

Tracey took a deep breath, the way a little kid might when he was launching into a long, involved lie. "Look, they found her with the needle in her arm, all the paraphernalia and shit, there's no proof—"

"You said it yourself, Corey didn't *do* heroin."

"Corey was an addict," he said, too loud. "I can't say what she would or wouldn't do if she was trying to get high."

"Well you seemed pretty convinced a few hours ago." If Gramma were still alive, she would have insisted on me inviting him into the house, partially because he was still a guest (though an annoying one) and partially because loud arguments shouldn't be conducted on the porch. I wasn't feeling too hospitable tonight, though.

"So I should just arrest him without any proof? We're not the secret police, Frannie."

"*Look* for fucking proof! Do your *duty* to those girls!"

He rubbed his face with his hands. I felt the briefest spark of pity, which was stifled as soon as he spoke. "Frannie, I can't go against the entire department."

I remembered the burning feeling around my neck and, almost worse, that unholy *knowing*. When I thought about Shayna feeling that . . . "Then you're gonna have to make peace with the fact that other people are gonna do what you can't," I said.

"But it doesn't have to be you, Frannie. This isn't your job."

"Well, I'm the only one who is going to do it, so—"

"Great. More of your martyr bullshit. That's helpful."

"What are you talking about?"

"I'm talking about you acting like the world is forcing you to be a doormat when it's not, Frannie. You just can't stop lying down. Your grandma didn't force you to basically drop out of school to take care of her and she sure as shit wouldn't have wanted you skip college to pay for this old farmhouse. The diner wouldn't collapse if you moved away and got a better job. Those are *your* choices, Frannie. Just yours."

I reeled back as though he had physically hit me. "Sure, I had a choice." My voice was shaking. I would never forgive myself if I started crying. "I had a choice between staying or leaving. Between abandoning people and caring for them. I mean, I can see how *you* would choose but some of us can't do that. We can't *be* that. You forget that the shit jobs still gotta get done by somebody."

"And if that job gets you killed? Don't you care about that?"

"Don't you care about the people who are dying because it's gone undone?"

"I spent today working a friend's death" he sat down on the porch swing. Somehow, it still managed to make him look small. "A girl I *knew*. I . . . can't do that for you. I can't . . . " he choked, "make arrangements or tell your family . . . "

I crossed the porch and sat next to him on the porch swing. Together, we stared out into the night.

"Matty showed me something," I said softly. "I can't explain it and I know it sounds crazy, but I think he showed me what . . . what it felt like. To have that happen to you, what Ray did to those women. And I can't sleep on that Tracey. I can't ignore it."

He reached out and took my hand. For a second, I thought he was going to try again to convince me to stop looking for Shayna, but instead he lifted my hand to his mouth and kissed the knuckles, where the strange fingernail marks still shone in angry half-circles. He looked at me and I knew two things: that he wanted my forgiveness and that he could not help me.

8

almost ignored my cell when it rang, about thirty minutes after I watched Tracey drive away. But who would I be if I ignored someone who might need something from me?

"Frannie? It's Daisy. Um, so I know it's not your night to work but it's crazy over here and I'm swamped."

I stood up. "Christine isn't there?"

Daisy sighed into the phone. "Well, she is but she brought her whole family for dinner. Half the town is here, Frannie. Most of the marching band, Doug and Kathleen, that whole church youth group, even

Ray Keene is here, having some big hurrah before he goes—"

"Ray Keene? He's there right now?" Tracey had mentioned before he left that he'd actually tried to locate Ray and was told that he was out on a run. "A run," my ass. He was skipping town, maybe dumping evidence.

"Yeah," I could practically hear Daisy roll her eyes. "He's buying people rounds of *pop* like he's some big shot." So he was in a good mood then. And why wouldn't he be? He'd just tied up one of his last loose ends.

I thought about what Tracey had said, about unassailable proof and about how the only way to get him was to ambush him when he wasn't looking.

"Okay, Daisy," I said, slow and clear. "I need you to do something really, really important for me."

• • •

I parked in back of the convenience store. I didn't

know if Ray Keene knew my car but I didn't want to take the chance. I certainly knew his rig, cherry-red and shiny, a more expensive machine than he should have had.

I kept looking in the diner windows as I moved through the parking lot. I knew from experience it would be virtually impossible for anyone to see me creeping around out here but I still walked in a crouch, hiding behind parked cars whenever I could. I'd asked Daisy to distract Ray however she could manage but I had no idea how long she could do that.

I stood before the cab of his truck, my heart lodged my throat like a too-ambitious bite of dinner. Right before I climbed up, I texted Tracey a short message. That, too, was a kind of timer because if he got out here and discovered what I was doing, he'd put a stop to it not matter what I had—or hadn't—discovered.

Behind the passenger side, there was a little quarter-window that looked likely. I remembered once how Devon had popped out a window like this, except it was on an ordinary truck (belonging to man who insisted we called him "Grampa Bill," despite the fact that he was forty and fucking our mother).

I pulled my jacket sleeve down over my hand on the off chance that the glass shattered and pressed as hard as I could on the bottom corner of the glass. To my relief, it popped out in one piece and bounced harmlessly off the fake-leather seat cover.

Inside, the truck smelled like the sticky, artificial sweeteners of an energy drink and also like a certain kind of particularly masculine body odor. There was a half-smoked cigarette languishing in the ash tray.

I popped the glove compartment first, where I found a nondescript handgun tucked into its holster. I reached out with the paper towels that I had brought along for this purpose and picked up the gun delicately, putting it into a plastic bag, which I had also brought with me. Contaminated evidence was worse than worthless.

When I lifted my hand to shut the glove box, I noticed a thread of what looked like hair twining around my fingers. I held it up to the dome light and I could see that it was blonde, peroxide-white. I re-opened the plastic bag and, as delicately as I could manage, dropped the hair inside with the gun.

I scrambled back into the bunk area, which was a stark contrast to the apartment that Ray had shared with Corey—a place for everything and everything in it's place. He had stripped his bed and folded the covers and the sheets on the end. He had stuck little hooks on the walls and hung a lanyard with what looked like extra keys from them as well. He had hung up a few shirts and a fluorescent green vest in a small recessed chamber next to the bed. I moved to examine them when something gleamed amongst the keys.

Underneath the lanyard there was a small gold chain. At the end there was a pendant, a big heart clustered with little fake diamonds. It seemed to me like something I would have worn when I was a kid.

I couldn't image an adult woman having it, let alone an adult man.

I unfolded the blankets with the tips of my fingers, a little bit afraid of what I was going to find. At first, there was nothing, just a pilled-up flannel blanket and an unzipped sleeping bag. Then came the sheet, cornflower blue except for a stain about the side of my hand that was deep brown and stiff to the touch.

I had seen ketchup stains and barbecue stains and wine stains and vomit stains and this was none of those. *He kept them here,* I thought. *He hurt them here and made them bleed. Maybe he even killed them here.*

There was nothing on the rest of the sheets, just this single, ominous stain. I tossed the now-loose blankets on the bunk and crouched down to peer underneath. Ray had tucked several plastic bins under the bed and they were almost entirely porn DVDs, with a few sad, worn magazines thrown in for variety, I supposed. I also found a small foil package like the ones I had seen burned out in Ray's apartment. I felt that familiar anger rise up in my chest. If the Sheriff's department had just *looked* . . .

I dug through the bin until I felt the flat of the plastic bottom and then, something cold. I pulled up a pair of very real looking handcuffs with more of that white-blonde hair trapped in the lock. Also at the bottom was a box made of thick paper with a floral design, like a gift box you might get at a nice department store.

Inside the box, there were pictures that looked very much the ones Corey had taken of her injuries. They were, I realized, taken with the same camera. But the woman—*women*—in these photos were completely unfamiliar to me. There was the woman with the white-blonde hair and another with curly hair. In one photo, I could clearly see the tattoo of a crown on her arm. Two brunettes who looked alike, one of them no more than thirteen or fourteen. An older woman with a long braid who looked directly into the camera as though she had seen me on the other side of it. There was something so eerie in her face, a kind of tired understanding, like she had always imagined that, somehow, some way, she was going to end up in front of that camera lens.

Underneath the photograph, there was more hair. Much more. I followed the white strands up to their roots, still connected to something that looked like a large scab, slightly curled in on itself. It was a piece of someone's scalp, skin and meat.

I took a deep breath and the sound of it filled my skull. Then, two things happened very fast: King, Doug's faithful old brown lab, started howling and my cellphone vibrated in my pocket. I didn't even need to check it to know exactly what it was—Daisy had failed and Ray was coming out to the parking lot.

I scrambled back to the driver's seat just in time to see Ray's face appear in the window. He was fumbling with the door, trying to get it unlocked. "What the fuck are you doing?" he yelled, his voice softened and diffused by the door between us.

I threw myself backward, navigating clumsily over the passenger seat armrests. I still had the photos clutched in one hand, though the hank of hair had fallen to the floor in the back. The door swung open and he came at me, head down like a human missile. He slammed his full weight against me, pressing us both into the passenger door. He kept snatching for the photos and I held them over my head, the most bizarre game of keep away I'd ever played.

Distantly, I heard someone scream and I thought it might have been Daisy.

Constrained by the interior of the truck, neither of us had our full range of movements and so our struggle was tiny, furtive and ineffectual. He kept hitting me with his free fists, little jabs that made one eye go black. I kicked my legs wildly, hitting the seats, the dashboard, the steering column and, occasionally, Ray himself.

"Are you crazy?" he demanded, batting at my flailing hands.

"Where's Shayna?" I shouted back.

"What the fuck are you talking about!"

"Her drawing! You had her drawing!"

He lost focus for a second, genuinely confused, and I took the opportunity to crack him on the side of the head with my fist. The blow didn't put him out or anything but it clearly rattled him. I pressed my advantage and reached for the passenger door handle. With an enormous roar, he leapt at me, tackling me and sending the both of us tumbling out the now-opened door and on to the pavement below.

I hit the ground first, him on top of me. I croaked once, like I was already dying and there was a moment of panic when I sucked for air but couldn't get any relief. My hands were crushed between us in the fall and so I couldn't fight Ray off when he put his hands around my throat, not just choking me but shaking my head, slamming it into the pavement. *THWACK!*

I had always imagined that when people said that your life flashed before your eyes when you died they meant the totality of your life, cradle on up.

THWACK!

Instead, all I could think was how stupid it all was.

THWACK!

I was dying, here in this parking lot at the hands of this asshole. How small it had been and what a waste. Maybe, I thought, the whole world a dark blur before me, Tracey had it right after all . . .

My breath came back in a huge rush. I saw a billion little pinpoints of light, blocking out the man's face above mine.

All I could feel was a strange spreading warmth, like warm water slowly saturating my shirt.

I looked up to see something bizarre, a little silvery point sort of like the tine of a fork protruding from Ray's neck about where his Adam's apple should have been. He gurgled at me and dark liquid swelled around the silver protrusion. His eyes were bright and blinking rapidly as though he were struggling mightily to understand what was happening to him.

I shoved him off me and rolled to the side. For a long minute, I just laid on the pavement. Cold from the ground filtered up from my back while his still-warm blood plastered my shirt to my chest. When I could focus enough to look around me, I could see Daisy standing above me, her hands hanging limply at her sides. She was sobbing, huge, hiccuping, uncontrollable sobs.

Beside me, Ray crawled miserably, one hand on his wounded throat the other offering him wobbly support. He made it a few feet and I managed to turn my head to watch him. He approached the small crowd of people who had emerged from the diner and I saw Doug and other folks I knew amongst their ranks.

Ray moved toward them slowly but doggedly as though he imagined that they were safety, they were life. If he could just reach them . . .

And he did, more or less. He got about three feet from Doug and Kathleen, who just looked at him. Kathleen was holding on to King's leash and every muscle in the old dog's body was stiff with rage. They *all* just looked at him, these local folk who knew exactly what he was.

And, as it had done for so long, Our Lady of the River's Mouth left Ray Keene to his own devices.

I got to my feet, feeling around the back of my head. It was slick with fluid and when I brought my palm around to look at it, my entire hand was red. "Are you dying?" Daisy sobbed. I automatically reached out to touch her shoulder and realized too late that I had touched her with my bloody hand, leaving a print on her uniform.

"Sorry," I muttered.

The police car approached with a long, sustained siren and a dizzying flash of lights. Almost before the car completely stopped, Tracey leapt out of it, running across the parking lot towards the rig and Daisy. And me.

"Frannie!" He took me by the shoulders and searched my face. "Are you hurt?"

"My head," I said, "is bleeding pretty good but I'll live."

He touched the back of my head and stared hard at the blood for a moment before enveloping me in a crushing hug. "Frannie," he muttered against the top of my head. "You are so, so dumb, Frannie," his voice was cracking.

He stepped back to look at me again and then he was kissing my face, kissing the places where I realized I must be cut up, either from getting hit or from the pavement and then he was kissing my mouth and maybe I kissed him back a little too but then I put my hands on his chest and pushed away from him.

"There's proof. He took pictures of them. Kept pieces of them, it's all in the truck."

Stuart was standing over Ray, who wasn't moving anymore. He was curled on his side and I could see for the first time where Daisy—Daisy!—had put a fish knife through his throat.

"I'm sorry," Daisy choked out. My bloody handprint looked so red on her shoulder. "He saw the light on in the truck and waited until I went in the back . . ."

Stuart stooped to examine Ray, putting two fingers to the side of his neck. "He's alive," Stuart said and he and Tracey exchanged dark looks.

"Take her to the hospital," Stuart said, nodding towards their squad car. "I'll call an ambulance for him. Eventually."

Epilogue

What hills, what hills, are those, my love?
That are so dark and low?
Those are the hills of Hell, my love
Where you and I must go
—*House Carpenter, Traditional*

I had a hairline skull fracture but no damage to my brain. Which was good because there are some who might tell you I can't afford to lose any more brain cells. Two of my ribs on my left side were cracked and I had a whole bunch of scrapes and bruises but, all things considered, I came out all right. A lot better than most women who had tangled with Ray Keene.

He was declared dead at the scene. Bled-out, apparently and the Sheriff's office declined to open an investigation. Witnesses said that Ray got into a fight—as he was known to do—with someone and got knifed. And Ray's killer? Well, he was a stranger, just passing through.

With Ray's death, everything else had gone quiet. People in town wanted nothing more than to forget about this whole sorry situation and that was exactly what they were doing, more or less.

I couldn't forget, though, and not just because of the bumpy stitches on the back of my head. There was nothing of Shayna in Ray Keene's truck and nothing else had turned up in the forest. Ray Keene was gone but Shayna was too and I couldn't help but feel that everything was . . . unfinished, somehow.

Tracey showed up about three weeks after I left the hospital, toting a small, soft-sided crate. "Let me in," he hollered at the door, "I'm bearing gifts and shit."

"What the hell is that, Tracey?"

"It's a dog," Tracey said, setting the crate down on the floor. "Someone left him tied up to an electric pole."

I bent over, peering through the small grille in the front. The puppy inside licked at the metal bars when he saw me, pawing at it in a friendly sort of way.

"It's a mutt, a pitbull mix I think. But with the size of those paws, he's gonna be a big boy."

"You got me a guard dog?" I stuck one finger through the wire and the entire crate shook as the dog vibrated with excitement.

"I brought you a *stray* dog," Tracey corrected. "Because taking care of strays is just about your favorite thing."

"Well, take him out of that thing at least. It looks like he's in Puppy Jail."

Tracey reached down and opened the door. The puppy bounded out immediately, leaping up to scrabble at my knees. I knelt beside him to give him a scratch and got a series of sloppy licks as a reward.

"He likes you."

"I don't need a protector." I rubbed the puppy's floppy grayish ears, softer than velvet.

Tracey sat down on the floor beside me. "Yeah, but you could use a friend."

We sat in silence for a little while, petting the puppy who wriggled in doggy ecstasy. "We got some results on that blood-stained blanket you found in Keene's truck," he said. "It wasn't Shayna's. It matched one of the other victims, one of the sisters."

I nodded, not sure exactly how to feel. I wasn't disappointed, really—I hadn't wanted Shayna's blood to be in Ray's truck—but that at least would have been something certain.

"And you know there's still a pretty good chance that Shayna just decided to move on. Maybe one of these days, you'll go out to your mailbox and find a postcard from her. Somewhere sunny next to the ocean."

I smiled because it was a nice thought but I just couldn't make myself believe it, not deep down in the part of me that had looked at Ray Keene and just *known*.

"You can't save everybody, Frannie," Tracey said, curling his arm around me and pulling me against him. We weren't exactly *together,* Tracey and me but since everything went down we hadn't been much apart either.

"I know." Since I was little, I'd been failing to save people, whether it was my mother or Gramma or Devon or even my poor little rat. "But I wanted to save her."

• • •

I went out to the forest after work, just before dark when everything was rosy and dull. I carried a steaming Styrofoam take-out box with me and Prince—the name I'd given to the puppy—ran out ahead of me, sniffing avidly.

I set the Styrofoam container on the ground in the clearing where the last woman was found. Prince gave it a thorough investigation before I shooed him away.

"I know this isn't your place," I said, talking at no one in particular. I didn't have whatever it was that let Matty communicate with the Lady, so I would have to rely on words and good intentions. "But I wanted . . . I wanted to thank you."

It had occurred to me that no one pulled the Lady's body out of the woods. No one was looking for her name or her people. Maybe she didn't even have people anymore. Maybe everyone who had ever loved her or missed her was dust now.

"I didn't know what you would like, so I brought pancakes. They're blueberry with the good honey on top." I knew I didn't have much to offer her, so I thought about what Shayna might have wanted, what any traveler wanted: a good meal and some good luck.

"I hope you get where you're going," I said, carefully setting down a paper cup full of coffee next to the container.

I figured that was about the best anyone could hope for in this world.

* * *

She just stood there and I guess she was saying something but she sounded all thin and muffled, like she was whispering into the wrong end of the microphone.

There was something, though, about the shirt that she was wearing. It was a thin, collared shirt with three-quarter sleeves and what I presumed to be her name—Frannie—embroidered over her heart. On her back in big letters it said "HIGHWAY 46 DINER" with a sketchy drawing of an enormous hamburger rooted on top of a flagpole. I had seen that before, what felt like a long time ago.

Yeah. The Highway 46 Diner. I had been there once, though the doors were shut with a chain through them and the windows were gray and impenetrable with dust. The big hamburger on a pole had been damaged with what looked like BB holes. The parking lot was empty and even the CLOSED sign in one window looked old.

I paced around the parking lot, weeds halfway up to my knees, hoping for a ride. I needed to get to the coast fast. In my memory, I can only feel the urgency like bile in my belly, but I cannot conjure up what exactly I thought was waiting for me out there.

A big red truck turned into the lot. The driver had seen me, fretting and pacing with my big bag on my back—everything that mattered to me then. His wheels were over-sized, they crunched the crumbling pavement all the way over to me.

I saw him first through the window. Late-twenties, early thirties, curly hair and big, sleepy stoner eyes. "You need a lift?" he asked me and we both knew that I did.

He told me his name was Matty. I gave him a name that was not my own. When he didn't take the turn out to the highway onramp, I must have looked how I felt. He must have seen the little tense spike of electric fear in me, because he tried to reassure me.

"I used to live around here," he told me. "I know all the shortcuts."

AUTHOR'S NOTE

Debbie Ackerman and Maria Johnson, fifteen-year-old high schoolers from Galveston, Texas, were having a good day. They'd gone shopping at the Galveston mall and then stopped on their way home for ice cream. They were seen later at that same ice cream store, getting into a white van.

The last time Opal Charmaine Mills's family spoke to her, it was when she called her brother, hoping to get a lift to a painting job she'd been offered. She was possibly going to take along her friend and occasional co-worker Cynthia Hinds.

When her brother told her he couldn't drive her, she assured him that she'd figure something out.

In 1989, Delphine Nikal's eighteen-year-old cousin Cecilia vanished from the modest town of Smithers, British Columbia and was still missing in 1990 when Delphine headed to Smithers herself for a day out with friends. Delphine lived with her family in Telkwa, B.C. There are a lot of towns like Telkwa along Highway Nineteen; remote, sparsely serviced, economically depressed and home to many Aboriginal people, there is minimal public transportation and many residents do not own a car. Most rely on rides from friends or family or even from strangers.

LaQuetta Gunther was only supposed to be gone for a little while, a couple of hours at most. She and her friend Stacey were going to stay up late, cooking a massive dinner—a Christmas Eve tradition that LaQuetta never missed, no matter what else was going on in her life. LaQuetta struggled with addictions and homelessness, sometimes working as a day laborer or a prostitute. She was known as someone who was tough and fierce but a loyal friend nonetheless.

LaQuetta was discovered a few days later, shot in the head and abandoned in an alley. She was the first of what police now believe is a series of murders—potentially more than twenty—linked to Interstate Four in Central Florida.

Debbie and Maria were found in a Texas City bayou, in an area near Interstate Forty-five that has come to be known as "the killing fields" for the sheer number of bodies that have turned up there in the last few decades. Opal and her friend Cynthia were both found in Washington's Green River, left there by Gary Ridgeway, who would later be dubbed "The Green River Killer" for his habit of leaving the bodies of his victims in and around that area.

Delphine Nikals has never been found, nor has her cousin. The area where she disappeared has acquired a macabre nickname: The Highway of Tears. Women like Delphine (Native, local, from working-class families) go missing there with a horrifying regularity. Figures differ but anywhere from nineteen to forty-some cases of missing or murdered women can be linked to that four-hundred-fifty-mile stretch of highway.

There is an FBI task force created specifically to address the phenomenon of serial murders linked to major thoroughfares in the United State, called the Highway Serial Killings Initiative. They have created a list of more than seven hundred fifty cases of murder they believe are linked and a similar list of more that four hundred fifty suspects with an unusually high proportion of truck drivers.

For someone who wants to kill people, trucking offers unparalleled opportunities to do so. Truckers are paid to move between states—between law enforcement jurisdictions—and they are alone virtually all of the time. They have a contained, mobile, private space, and ample access to vulnerable populations.

These women are often living what law

enforcement calls "high-risk lifestyles." Which means, to some degree, we as a society and law enforcement in particular are not shocked when these people go missing. When a smiling young college student or a stay-at-home mom vanishes, it is treated as an emergency. When a prostitute or a homeless person vanishes, it is unremarkable and something that may very well resolve "on its own."

There is a pragmatism in this, roughly half a million missing persons reports are made each year and many of them are people who are "voluntary missing"—adults who simply dropped out of contact for reasons of their own. People who struggle with addiction and move around a lot may go long periods of time without checking in and it doesn't necessarily mean they've been harmed.

However, people in these "high risk" categories simply *do* get murdered at a higher rate than college students and stay-at-home. It seems counterintuitive to treat their cases as *less* important because they are more likely to actually encounter foul play.

Not that these are easy cases to solve. A traveling killer can pick up a person in one state, murder them in another, and leave their body in a third, involving countless law-enforcement agencies. By selecting victims who are often estranged from family and have friends amongst a community deeply wary of police, the killer can ensure that their victim will not be reported missing until much later, if ever. Just because it is difficult, however, doesn't mean that these cases shouldn't be investigated as aggressively as the most recent missing child or pretty, young white woman. These women were human beings, just trying to get where they were going. Instead, someone interrupted them, stole everything they had, and abandoned them in some lonesome place.

I would like to leave you with just one more story:

Ellen Smith was, by the standards of 1890s North Carolina, living a high-risk lifestyle. She was poor (a maid at a local hotel) and she was young (just seventeen), a census lists her as "mulatto" and she was likely visibly mixed race. She also may have been mentally impaired. Most dangerous of all, she was entangled with an older man with a bad reputation: Peter DeGraff, a twenty-something who worked at the same hotel.

DeGraff was not the kind of boy you bring home to mother but, according to that same period census, Ellen Smith was an orphan. She and DeGraff had been in a relationship for more than a year and some accounts suggest they even had a child together who died shortly after birth.

No one knows exactly what happened between the two of them. Some have suggested that Ellen tried to break away from DeGraff, sending him a "Dear John" letter that infuriated him. Others have described the opposite situation: DeGraff, after impregnating the teenage Ellen, tried to move on to other women. But Ellen, devastated by the loss their child, and possibly mentally incapable of fully understanding the situation, pursued him.

Whatever the reason, Peter DeGraff likely knew exactly what he was going to do when he wrote Ellen a letter summoning her to a secluded spot in the forest. Ellen, either out of hope or pity, went and it was there that he murdered her, shooting her from such close range that powder burns were visible on her dress when she was found shortly thereafter.

It didn't take a Sherlock Holmes to figure this one out. DeGraff's contentious relationship with Smith was common knowledge locally and the man himself fled after the murder, hiding unsuccessfully in a nearby town. The public soon developed a fascination with this case and no small part of that was due to Peter DeGraff, who adopted a flamboyantly repentant persona. Nevertheless, his last words on the gallows were a sober warning to avoid "whiskey, cards and bad women," implying that Ellen herself had somehow driven him to murder her.

The intense interest in this case gave rise to what is often called a "murder ballad." Capitalizing on the public fascination with tales of murder and mayhem—which is about as old as murder itself—these songs imparted facts of the case along with plenty of lurid details to satisfy the most ghoulish listener. The songs also usually offered some warning for the listener.

Versions of "Poor Ellen Smith" chided young women not to be promiscuous and warned young men to avoid vice of all types. Many are sung from the perspective of DeGraff, either professing his innocence or wondering, as he did in real life, why he had killed a woman that he "loved."

The real reason, of course, had nothing to do with the perils of gambling or Ellen's personal conduct. Peter DeGraff murdered his erstwhile lover because he believed that he was entitled to do so. He thought that his desires—whether they be to punish Ellen for leaving him or to simply make her go away—were more important and more valuable than her life.

Ellen doesn't speak in any of the well-known versions of the ballad. Her killer gets plenty of space to mourn—or deny—his crime and how it means the gallows for him. That, the song implies, is as great (or greater) a tragedy as Ellen's murder.

Ellen's most significant appearance is in the first stanza, where she is discovered "shot through the breast, lying cold on the ground." She exists in song and story and American folklore as a body. She's a moral, an example, a cautionary tale, a legend, a myth, a ghost, a corpse.

But that was not always true. Ellen Smith was a real, live person. She had thoughts and fears, she knew love and joy and sorrow (more than her share, in fact). She was more than the caricature of her that Peter DeGraff constructed and she was much more than a body "lying cold on the ground." She had value, she had worth, and she deserved better.

They all did.